"Do you know how old I am?"

"We're not ageists here," Jill said.

"I'm old enough to be your grandmother."

"Not if you're still working at Safeway, you're not. My grandma's got the old-age pension."

"When I was young, we had some respect for old people."

"Everybody should respect everybody," Angel said.

"I have every respect for you," Alice said with dignity. "Even about sex."

"You know what you should do, Alice?" Angel asked. "It's not too late . . . is come out."

"Come out?" Alice demanded. "Of where? This is my house after all. You're just renting the main floor. Come out? To whom? Everyone I know is dead!"

Theme for Diverse Instruments

JANE RULE

The Naiad Press, Inc.
1990

Printed in the United States of America

Cover design by Pat Tong and Bonnie Liss
    (Phoenix Graphics)
Typeset by Sandi Stancil

Library of Congress Cataloging-in-Publication Data

Rule, Jane.
    Theme for diverse instruments / by Jane Rule.
        p.   cm.
    ISBN 0-941483-63-0
    I. Title.
PR9199.3.R78T5   1990
813'.54--dc20   89-48973
                                                                  CIP

for Helen

WORKS BY JANE RULE

1964   *Desert of the Heart**
1970   *This is Not for You**
1971   *Against the Season**
1975   *Lesbian Images*
1975   *Theme for Diverse Instruments**
1977   *The Young in One Another's Arms**
1980   *Contract with the World**
1981   *Outlander**
1985   *A Hot-Eyed Moderate**
1985   *Inland Passage and Other Stories**
1987   *Memory Board**
1989   *After the Fire**

*Available from The Naiad Press.

Contents

In the Basement of the House

I can't go back to a women's lib meeting even if he thinks I should. When we break up into small discussion groups, rapping about kids or housework or sex, everybody else says things like, "As a mother . . ." or "As a female rake . . ." or "As a lesbian . . ." I can't start out as an anything. It's like being the only kid at camp without labels sewed in my underpants. I could say that, I guess, and nobody would mind, but it doesn't help *me* any. He's the only one I can talk to. I don't feel like it much, though, or, when I do, there isn't time. Maybe I only do when I know I can't. Like making love or thinking about it. I'd rather think about it. Not about the way it is. Nobody gets around to that. Everybody says, "Now let's really talk about sex," and pretty soon we're all talking about money or freedom or baby sitters. Well, the girl with the deep voice did say laying girls was fun, but then someone else got off onto whether or not that was really male chauvinist stuff, and we were into politics. When Sharon said, "What's wrong with being an easy lay?", it was just like when we talked about long term relationship: half an hour defining terms, and then

1

somebody got into her bastard gynecologist who wanted to know how many different guys screwed her and what color they were. I did find out what a cone biopsy was that night, but the next day I read an article in *Redbook* that make it a lot clearer.

Wanting me to go to women's lib is the same as wanting me to sleep around. It's like he's got this idea in his head about freedom. He's not comfortable with it unless I'm free, too. But he doesn't screw around . . . except with me, and he doesn't go to meetings to talk about it. I don't think he talks about it with anybody, except maybe with her. I don't know about that. Funny the things you just don't know, even living in the same house. Maybe it's just me, though. Maybe almost everyone else would know.

Sometimes I think I do learn something at those meetings. That night everyone was talking about the myth of vaginal orgasm and Masters and Johnson, I wondered if that was why I only ever really come when he's licking me. But I could come the other way, or it feels like I could. I just don't want to. I don't know why I don't. There's too much going on for him then. Or I really do think coming with him would make me pregnant, pill or not. I know that's not true, even if Norman Mailer believes it. Germaine Greer says coming with a full cunt is nicer. I don't know what all that stuff has to do with being liberated. But he does like screwing better than I do. It's harder for him, but he gets more out of it, as if he'd really accomplished something. Still, I can't see that it's his fault. I didn't like any of it at first. It was like getting used to Sarah's dirty diapers. Now I don't even take a bath afterwards. I like to sleep with his smell or my smell or whatever it is.

I worry about her, more than anything. I think I really like her better, but isn't it natural that I would? I can identify with her. I can imagine how she feels. But I don't know anything about how she feels. I thought I was going to throw up or faint or scream that time I walked into the kitchen and saw her pulling her hand out of another woman's pants. It doesn't bother me at all now. Oh, I knock or whistle or somehow let her know I'm around, but for her sake, not mine. At first I thought, so that's why he wants to screw me, but now I'm not even sure he knows. And what if she does it because he screws me? She does know about that. That's what she meant when she said, "If you don't really like everything that goes along with the job, quit. Or if you do, don't get up tight about it." Maybe I like her better because she can say things like that, which make more sense than all his worry about freedom and guilt. He doesn't know how to be that kind of honest. I never hear him encouraging her to go to women's lib. If we both went, he'd have to stay home with the kids. He's nice to the kids though. He really listens to them, a lot more than she does, probably more than I do, too. And he's gentle with them. She and I do more rough housing with David than he does. So who's making a man of David? And she doesn't even want a man, and I like him because he's so gentle. When one of the kids is sick, he's better than either of us. He doesn't get up in the night, of course, but she says, "He sleeps like a human being, not like a dog, the way you and I do." It's true, I have my head off the pillow at any sound in the night. It's not just because I sleep in the basement, all of their noises right on top of me. I slept that way at home, too, in the attic. It's being the oldest or a girl.

It really was funny when that woman said, "I dig raising kids. I really do. Only two things I miss: a good, long uninterrupted sleep and a good, long uninterrupted crap." Never had either to miss. Will I sometime? If I get through

3

college, if I get a real job, if I move out of this house?

"The trouble with pets and husbands is that they never grow up and leave home." When she says things like that, I do feel guilty, and I'm not sure why. Am I sorry for her? She's got a good job of her own, and, in the last couple of months, she got rid of the woman who was hanging around so much and is into a new kind of thing, somebody she's really friends with. I like to see them together, but, of course, I stay out of the way as much as I can. I am getting paid to watch the *kids*.

She's attractive. I didn't use to know what that meant. It isn't good looking, though she is that, her hair particularly. It's good feeling, good vibes. I understand why people like to be around her. Sometimes I'd like to ask him straight questions, lawyer's questions, like, "Why don't you screw your wife?" Maybe he does. Maybe she doesn't want him to.

He's not attractive. One of those thin men with a watermelon pot, thin hair, thin mouth. Even his voice is thin. But that's not it. Nobody ever knows he's in the room. That his body is. His head is there all right, and people like his head. If she came into my room with a bunch of books for me, I'd know in a minute what she was there for. She wouldn't even have to smile in a certain way or touch me. Maybe women have that and men just don't. Or he's different from other people. Nobody talks about being attractive at women's lib. I couldn't talk about it.

"Speaking as a baby sitter who lives in the basement and gets screwed by the boss . . ." and I'd have to say which one, not just because of the real possibilities here, but because that sort of thing is expected. I couldn't call him 'my lover'. At first he was like a very gentle gynecologist, really interested in my body, only he wasn't feeling around for lumps. Then he wanted me to be interested in his, as if I were taking a course in it and might need to write up a lab report. Once I got over being afraid he'd pee in my mouth, I didn't mind sucking him, and I think he likes it that way, too, not having to think about anybody else. Just a little while ago, when he came in my mouth, I started peeing, right on the floor, and I didn't want to stop. Sometimes I wonder if sex is just learning not to be embarrassed about anything, letting it all go. So why housebreak Sarah? I'm not serious, and nobody in this house is uptight about housebreaking anything. I clean it all up, dog, kids, the lot.

I couldn't say any of that. It makes me sound like an animal. Or something worse. I haven't read enough Freud to know what people would call me, even if he is wrong. Like when I read Reich's *Sexual Revolution*. Why does he think that if you let little kids pee around and play with themselves and each other, they'll grow up to live in communes without any trouble? Serial monogamy, 100 percent heterosexual. I don't understand what I read. If it's supposed to have something to do with me, I don't.

I'm sorry I don't think he's attractive. I don't know why I care. He's another human being. He's gentle, and he's kind. He likes to do the right thing. He talks about that a lot. But what is the good of people talking to each other if they can't tell the truth? I get scared about what will happen. Nobody at women's lib ever seems to be scared. Let it all hang out, get your head straight, be liberated.

If I ever said it like it is . . . I know my label. "Speaking as a slave . . ." that's what they'd all think. I'm a wage slave, a student slave, diddled by the lord of the manor just like some Victorian governess, and I even clean up dog shit, never mind the kids. It doesn't make me mad. Mostly I don't even mind. But it isn't safe. Sometimes, when I hear him coming down the basement steps, I pretend it's her instead, and she's got a gun, and she's going to kill me, and then I'm really relieved and glad to see him, even though I know all along it's silly. I like her better than I do him. But I'm not comfortable with her. I'm always getting out of her way.

I'd like to go some place and do something that didn't make me feel guilty. I did try to tell him that women's lib for me was just another guilt trip, but I didn't understand it well enough myself to make him understand. He started talking about good guilt. If I felt guilty about not really taking myself seriously enough, not respecting my own mind, that was good guilt and I should face it. I get really embarrassed when he tells me what a fine mind I have. He needs to think so; otherwise he's just another guy trying to forget he's going bald. It would be better for me if my psych prof thought I had a good mind. He's never raised his eyes high enough to see that I've got a head. I don't want to pass psych on the size of my tits, and I wish I could figure out whether it's wearing a bra or not wearing a bra that turns men off. Can't ask something like that at a meeting. Nobody else knows either. What's so really bad about being a guy trying to forget he's going bald? Why would he be ashamed of screwing somebody ignorant and ordinary? He loves his kids. They're ignorant and ordinary. He probably doesn't think so. Can't. Maybe that's why he can listen so well. He's hearing all sorts of amazing things. When I was mad about getting the curse (I'm not supposed to call it that; it's unliberated) and said I wished I could give all that blood every month to the red cross, he told me I was an original thinker. Seriously! Would some guy figure out a way to do it and get famous? I don't even know what you'd have to major in.

Maybe part of it is that I'm younger than most of the others. I don't have their experience. Sex is still a big thing for me because I don't know much about it. If I could find

6

out whether or not most girls pee like that, I maybe wouldn't be scared I'm abnormal. Old people go back into second childhood. They put Granddad in a home when he began to lose control of himself, 'foul himself', Mother said. What if I have a senile bladder at eighteen? He liked it, but how do I know he's not some sort of pervert? Or telling me just to make me feel good? I tell him things to make him feel good, but I know when I'm doing it. Sometimes I'm not sure he does. He'd have to think I was attractive whether I am or not.

I couldn't let some kid screw me now. I wouldn't know what to do. If I don't do anything with him and just lie there, like the first time, he says it's very passive, and that's bad, but how do I know which things he's taught me are okay and which aren't? I could be really weird. If he doesn't know his own wife is queer — and I don't think he does — how would he know whether I was or not? Maybe somebody else could tell in a minute. I wouldn't show anyone else the way I showed him how I did it to myself. I didn't mind. He only wanted to see what I liked, but somebody else might know from that. She doesn't ever come on to me. Wouldn't she if I were?

"Please, could somebody tell me, if my landlady doesn't want to lay me, does that prove I'm straight or just unattractive?"

Maybe she doesn't because of him. Maybe she only likes people her own age. There's no way I'm going to find out about that at a meeting. There's no way I'm going to find out. I don't want to know.

Nobody in that room ever comes out and says they're scared to death they won't get married or will marry some guy who isn't really interested in them and is always off screwing some kid in the basement. Am I the only one who is? If I feel so sorry for her, why do I let him do it? She doesn't seem to care. I'm scared of her. I don't think she's going to shoot me. I make that up to have something I can imagine to be scared about. These last couple of months she's been so happy she has a hard time even getting irritated. What if she left him? Do women ever just go off with each other? But she couldn't take the kids. And I couldn't stay here if she wasn't here. It wouldn't look right. I wouldn't want to anyway. I think one of those women at the meeting did leave her husband and go live with another woman. When I asked him about women loving women, he laughed and said that was for flat chested school girls. I should feel sorry for him. At least she knows. She lives in the real world. He doesn't. He wouldn't know how.

If I just didn't have to think about it, if I just didn't have to go to all those meetings, maybe I'd stop being so scared. They all talk as if there weren't any danger, as if nobody ever got really mad, as if there weren't any laws. She could divorce him because of me, take his kids and his money and the house, everything. But liberated people don't do things like that. She wouldn't. But what about him? Wouldn't he go crazy if she tried to leave him and he knew why? He's gentle, and he's kind, and he's just afraid of going bald. But if losing his hair makes him screw his babysitter, what would he have to do if he lost his wife?

All I want to do is get through college and then find some nice, ordinary guy to marry me. I'll do my own baby sitting. We won't have a basement. What if it happens anyway? If somebody is afraid of losing his hair and somebody else is queer . . . are all women queer? Do they turn queer? What else could she do? The men are all after kids like me. She's not going to run after boys; she couldn't kid herself they were original thinkers, and she'd be bored. So what's left?

8

One thing I wish I had the guts to tell him: you send me to women's lib meetings much longer and I'm not going to be lying here making up her footsteps coming down the stairs to kill me. I'm going to be praying she's coming down the stairs to love me. And one thing I wish I had the guts to tell all of them is, if that's what women's liberation is all about, some of us may get killed for it, and I wasn't socialized like that. I'm too young to die.

It isn't funny. I shouldn't be living in this basement at all. There must be a basement somewhere else that's different, where I could just do my work and hole in until it's over. All I really need to figure out is how to use my very ordinary head and keep my tits out of my classwork and my landlord's mouth. I don't need to go to meetings for that. I just have to get out of here.

But what about her? What if he doesn't like the next one? What if the next one said something? She's not that careful. What if the next one was attractive? To her. Oh, shit! shit! Why do I have to live through all this shit and then all the marriage and baby shit before . . . before a woman like her would look at me. She can't make me up the way he does. I'm just a kid. What do my tits mean to her? She's got her own. She isn't afraid of losing her hair or her husband. I'm scared. I'm just too scared to love her. I won't be able to for years.

If he makes me go back to another one of those meetings, I'm going to tell him I won't. I'll move. I don't want to be liberated. There's got to be another way out.

My
Father's House

"Dicky, please can I come up now?" Maly called from her place among the wood shavings at the bottom of the basement window well. "Dicky? . . . Dicky, haven't I been in prison for twenty years yet?"

Dicky was walking slowly and carefully away from her, stepping from joist to joist across the foundation of the new house. He moved not directly across but in a pattern that honored the doorways which, when the walls were up, would be the passageways through this space. His hands were in his back pockets, and he was whistling his own monotone version of the "Star Spangled Banner."

"Dicky?"

"Maybe you've been in for six minutes. . . maybe," he called back when he had finished his tune.

"But there're bugs down here," she protested, pulling her scabbed knees as far up under her chin as she could and peering down between them at her white cotton pants and the shavings. "Black ones."

"Bed bugs," Dicky answered. He was on the far side of the foundation by now and was looking down into the dark basement, then back over his walk, admiring his own skill. "Prisons always have bedbugs. They stink if you squash them; so be careful. I'd have to burn all your clothes."

"Dicky, please? I didn't mean to walk through the wall, honest. I didn't know it was a wall. You said before it was the back door."

"I never did. The back door goes out of the kitchen. You walked right through the dining room wall."

Maly sighed and settled against the cold cement to wait a little longer. After a moment, she called to him again.

"What do you want?" he asked patiently. He was walking back across the joists, quickly this time.

"Daddy said last night that there were glass doors in the dining room, I heard him."

"That's in the house on Circle Drive. He showed me the plans for this one last week, and there isn't any door except in the kitchen."

"Maybe I climbed out the window," Maly suggested.

"It's a picture window. It doesn't open. You walked through the wall." Dicky was balancing on one foot, staring down into the basement. "Now shut up or I'll put you in solitary confinement."

"What's that?"

"Well, it's a place they put convicts. . ." Dicky hesitated. Like a spider spinning a web, he had finally moved back to the center of the network of joists and stood now looking out over the foundation, the vast reality of the small, accurate blueprint his father had shown him. He was very still, as he was when he watched his father build careful models out of balsa wood, the joists tiny and frail and perfect, cut with a razor, set in place with tweezers. Piece by piece, the fragile structure grew, and, as Dicky watched, the palms of his hands ached and itched just the way they did when he felt the ribs of a new-born kitten under his fingers. Now, at the center, the deep, black basement beneath him, he saw gigantic hands swing two-by-tens like toothpicks into place, saw the bones of the walls like prison bars go up all around him until he was in a cage, the rib cage of a huge animal. His heart pumped thick blood into his ears. And as the huge, quiet hands lifted rafters into place, the scaffolding black before the sun, Dicky cried out, "I am the King!"

"Of what?" Maly grumbled, bored with the bugs and the scabs on her knees.

The cage dissolved. The sun was mild on the new lumber piled in the lot.

"Of everything," Dicky said, but he was walking away from the center out toward the edge where Maly was imprisoned. "Do you ever think," he asked, peering down at her, "that you're inside a house?"

Maly twisted her head around to see Dicky, but his head was only a black patch against the sun, like a large, black jaw breaker. She pulled her nose down and caught her bottom lip between her teeth.

"I mean," Dicky said, "sort of built in and people don't know?"

"You mean, stuck in the wall?"

"Well, not exactly in the walls."

"You mean, like in the bathroom? Only they can't see you?"

"No, not like that."

Maly looked back down at her knees because the sun had spotted her eyes with dozens of tiny black jaw breakers.

"No," Dicky said again, "No, just being there, really being there."

"Oh." But, as Maly saw Dicky in the finished house, scuffing and whistling and making games, she couldn't imagine people not knowing he was there, and it made her sad to think of him in somebody else's family, as if he were an orphan. "I guess so."

"Prisoner released for special guard duty," Dicky said suddenly.

Maly uncrumpled her legs slowly and painfully. When she stood up, her head was just above the top of the window well, and she was looking directly into the pile of lumber. She put her hands on the ledge and felt the rough grains press into the palms as she hoisted herself out. Finally she stood above ground, rubbing her hands flat against her stomach to get rid of the small, dark dents in the skin.

"Stand by the lumber pile," Dicky ordered, as he jumped down off the foundation and walked toward the edge of the lot.

Maly looked after him and saw another boy, standing very still on the sidewalk. Maly climbed up on the lumber pile to watch. Dicky walked right up to him. They were just the same height, but Dicky's hair was yellow and the boy's hair was black. Maly thought of two boys who were still just spaces between lines in her coloring book and decided that one would be yellow, the other black.

"You're on private property," Dicky said, not unkindly, only to inform.

"Your house?" the boy asked, looking past Dicky at the foundation.

"My father's house," Dicky said. "He's building it."
"Oh."

"You want to look at it?"
"Sure."

Dicky walked back across the lot, the boy following him. Maly climbed off the lumber pile and went out to meet them.

"What's your name?" she asked.

"Ivy."

"Ivy?" Maly frowned, while Dicky began to climb back up onto the foundation. "How old are you?"

"Eight."

"Dicky's eight. I'll be six pretty soon."

"How soon?"

"Why are you Ivy?"

"Because that's my name."

"Well, come on if you're coming," Dicky called, standing above them. "Climb up there." He pointed to a keg of nails he had used.

Ivy boosted himself up onto the pile of lumber and then stepped onto the keg of nails. He hesitated for a moment before he jumped across the foundation. When he stood safely on the edge, he turned back to Maly.

"Aren't you coming?"

"I can't. I can't reach. Anyway, Dicky won't let me."

"Why not?"

"I walked through the wall."

"There isn't any wall," Ivy said, looking around him.

"It's a sort of game," Dicky said impatiently. "I show her where the walls go, and, if she walks through one, I put her in prison. You can come up, Maly, if you want to. Come around in back and I'll pull you up."

Dicky began his slow journey across the joists, through the imagined rooms, while Maly ran around the side of the house to meet him. Ivy paused, looking down into the deep hole of a basement between the boards. Then he began to walk very cautiously around the cement frame of the foundation. Dicky turned around.

"You're supposed to walk across, the way I did."

"I know," Ivy answered, watching his step. "I just want to begin over there instead of over here."

Maly had arrived at the place of the kitchen door. Dicky reached down to take hold of her outstretched hands. He braced his feet where board met cement and swung her up beside him. They stood together, watching Ivy.

"He's walked through all the walls, hasn't he?" Maly whispered.

"Yeh," Dicky answered, his mouth tight at one corner, as it always was when he was deciding about something.

"Maybe he doesn't know," Maly suggested.

"Maybe."

Ivy had come round the last corner of the foundation and was walking toward them. His face was mottled. He put his hands, which he had been carrying like full glasses of water, into his pockets as he stopped next to Maly. Then he looked out across the foundation, rocking a little from his knees.

"It isn't a very big house," he said.

"Well," Maly began, standing between the boys, nearer Dicky than Ivy, "the house fits on top."

"I know that. I just said it was a little house."

"That's because you can't see the walls. You walked through the outside walls," Dicky said.

"There aren't any walls."

Dicky stood, his mouth slightly open, gazing out over the foundation. "I'll race you across."

Ivy's fists tightened in his pockets, pulling his pants tight over his hip bones.

"Why don't we play house?" Maly suggested.

"Okay," Ivy agreed. "Okay, let's. You be. . ."

Dicky hopped out on one foot from joist to joist, his eyes careful and shallow from board to board so that he did not seem to see at all the deep, black pit beneath him. At the center, he stood on both feet, and looked down. "It's black down there," he called. "And there are snakes." He looked back at Ivy.

"There aren't any snakes."

"Come and see."

"I don't want to. I know there aren't any snakes."

"You're scared."

Ivy stood a moment very still, looking at Dicky. Then he took one step out onto a joist, another, then a third, until he was out over the pit far enough so that he couldn't step back to safety. He hardly looked where he stepped, and he did not look down. He kept his eyes on Dicky out there in the center of this big foundation.

"Watch out for snakes," Dicky called and then laughed.

Ivy involuntarily looked down. He swayed from his knees, standing with both feet on one board. The huge, dark hole, shadowed with fallen boards and pools of water, opened beneath him like a dungeon, like a world under water, like sleep, the life of roots and snakes and dead men's arms wailing up toward him like tears. He was weighted, dragged by fear. And above him the whole vast sky watched as if he must fall in the full sight of the sun into darkness, out of this frail world, this terrible world of unmade houses, of nowhere to step that wasn't as tentative, as dangerous, as openly unfinished as where he stood now, swaying, dizzy, sick.

"You have to be careful, Ivy," Maly said, standing beside him and taking his hand, "or you'll walk through the living room wall and have to be in prison. Put your other foot here."

Ivy shifted his weight, braced now on two joists. He looked across at Dicky. "There aren't any snakes," he said.

"I know," Dicky answered, walking over to them. "I was just kidding you."

Slowly the three together walked across the foundation, careful to move from room to room through the proper doors.

"Look how little the bathroom is, Ivy." Maly said, "Doesn't it look little?"

"Rooms without walls look small," Dicky explained. "Even with walls they look small without furniture."

"Yeh," Ivy said. He stood uneasily straddling darkness. "Say, I know a place to play. You want to see a really good place to play?" He was asking Dicky.

"Where?"

"Near. I'll show you." Ivy looked very quietly at Dicky.

"Well, okay."

"We have to be home at five," Maly reminded.

"It isn't far."

They stood for a moment.

"I'll race you to the edge," Dicky said.

Grimly, Ivy nodded, and they set out, Dicky jumping from joist to joist until he was in stride, then taking the joists two at a time. Ivy, head down, hands out ready to grab, wobbled and stumbled across with Maly close behind him. Dicky reached the concrete long before Ivy, watched him come, and caught Ivy in his arms just as he lept, misjudging the final distance to safety. They rocked together for a moment, then steadied on the edge.

"Boy," Dicky laughed, friendly, "you sure need practice."

"Boy!" Maly said.

"Let's go." Ivy broke away from Dicky roughly. He jumped down onto the keg of nails, from there to the lumber pile and onto the ground.

18

Dicky lowered Maly to the keg, then jumped past her to the lumber pile. When they were on the ground, they had to run to catch up with Ivy, who walked quickly as if he were going some place alone. Maly fell in step beside him. Dicky walked by her, scuffing his feet on the grass that grew in the parking strip. Maly wished there were a girl in the picture in her coloring book.

"Hey, Ivy," Dicky called as he stopped on the sidewalk and caught Maly's arm before she could follow Ivy across the lawn, "that's a church."

"I know."

"Well, you can't play in a church."

But Ivy kept walking until he reached the steps. Then he turned. "Well, aren't you coming?"

"It's a church," Dicky said again, walking slowly toward Ivy.

"This is *my* father's house."

"Your dad's a minister?"

"That's right."

"Oh." Dicky looked at Ivy and then at the church.

"It's God's house," Maly said as she began to look around her on the lawn, "so I have to have a hat." She found a large, dry magnolia leaf, picked it up and tried it on, but, as she turned her head to have Dicky's approval, the leaf floated back to the ground. She picked it up again, this time clipping it carefully under her bobby pin. "Okay," she said.

"Okay what?" Dicky retorted.

"Okay, I'm ready."

"I don't think. . ."

"Oh, come on," Ivy interrupted impatiently. "It's a great place to play. No one's in there."

"You sure?"

"Come and see." Ivy ran up the stairs and opened one of the great doors.

Maly went first, vaguely formal in her hat, on her toes, her head forward and tilted at the darkness. "Cold," she murmured, pushing her short skirt down against her thighs. "Hey, Dicky," she whispered without turning round to him, "it's cold."

Dicky didn't answer, but she felt him crowd against her to make room for Ivy who had come in and shut the door. They stood, pressed against each other in a small, warm huddle, in the gloom of the open vestibule. Before them, far down the center aisle, high on the altar, the cross caught and held a line of late orange sunlight.

"Go on," Ivy said.

"Where?" Maly asked.

"Haven't you ever been in a church before?"

"Of course we have," Dicky answered, forcing his voice above a whisper.

"Do you want to see the altar?"

"Sure."

Ivy pushed past them and walked down the aisle. Maly followed him. Dicky came last, looking up at the stained glass windows, behind them to the rafters fading into darkness overhead. Twice he stumbled against Maly. The second time she turned, annoyed.

"So watch where you're going," she whispered.

"So hurry up," he whispered back.

Ivy did not bother to open the gate. He vaulted the communion railing and jumped up the altar steps two at a time. Maly and Dicky stopped before the railing, uncertain.

"Open it, if you want," Ivy said. He was standing by the altar.

"Why is there a gate?" Maly said.

"Because this is where God lives," Ivy answered in a matter-of-fact voice. "The gate keeps sinners out of His house."

"What are sinners?"

"Bad people. Grownups."

"What happens," Dicky asked, "if they get in?"

"They don't get in."

"But what would happen if they just did?"

"They'd just fizzle up and die."

"Like slugs," Maly said, swinging on the railing, "when you pour salt on them."

"I don't believe you," Dicky said, looking up at Ivy.

"Then you're a sinner."

"I am not."

"Come on up here and see."

Dicky stood for a moment, looking at Ivy, then suddenly swung himself over the communion rail and stood on the bottom step of the altar, waiting for the flash of lightning from the cross, waiting to feel himself shrivel and melt. Nothing happened.

"I was kidding you," Ivy said. "But sinners would fizzle up and die."

Dicky swung back over the rail and stood beside Maly. He was not very comfortable.

"My father saves sinners," Ivy said.

"How?" Maly asked.

"Well. . ." Ivy hesitated. "You be the sinners, and I'll be the minister. I'll show you."

"Okay," Maly said. "What do we do?"

"Just stay there." Ivy stood down just before the cross. "You are the damned," he said, his voice curiously resonant. "All the unbelievers of the world are damned, and, when the Day of Judgment comes, when everyone in the world must enter God's house or die, you will fizzle up and die, like a snuffed candle, like a wisp of smoke, like a slug." Ivy was into his part. Below him stood the sinners, the unbelievers, almost damned, but his heart was huge with love for them, with pity and tenderness. He gathered up their ignorance and their wickedness into his voice, into his arms, which he raised high and wide above his head. He did not want them to die, to fall forever into the pit of wailing roots and snakes and arms. He wanted them to come into the kingdom of heaven with him.

"Suffer little children to come unto you. Suffer them. Heal them. Do not snuff them out. Do not pour the salt of your tears on them and fizzle them away. Bring them away from wickedness. Give them your body and blood to eat. Come all ye. . ." and here Ivy turned toward the vast congregation, toward the miserable sinners at the communion railing ". . . who are heavy laden . . ." Then he turned back and knelt before the altar. "Dear Lord, we do not presume. . ."

Maly knelt down and peered at Ivy through the bars of the communion railing. Dicky knelt awkwardly beside her.

"Hey, Ivy," Maly whispered, wanting to interrupt but not to disturb him. "Hey, Ivy." But Ivy was deep in prayer.

Dicky bit the white knuckles of his fist, which clenched the communion railing. Over his head in the vast, deep gloom, he heard the whir of wings like the breathing of giants or huge, black angels. And God was everywhere in this terrible house. He walked behind Dicky through invisible doors. He stood before Dicky on the other side of an invisible wall. Dicky did not know the rules. He might walk through that wall he couldn't see and be made to drink blood like a vampire in a black dungeon or be burned to death. He wanted to get up and run out of this place, back into the sun, back into the world of houses he knew, but he could not move. God was everywhere.

"Hey, Ivy!" Maly finally called in a loud voice.

Ivy turned on one knee and looked down at her. "What?" he said, vaguely irritated and then a little embarrassed.

"I want to know, what do we do?" She rested her cheek against one of the iron bars and absent-mindedly licked it with her tongue.

"What do you mean?"

"While you're doing. . ." she hesitated, "that."

Ivy leaned back, bracing his foot comfortably against the step below him. "Oh, you're supposed to be saved."

"How?"

"Well, you take communion."

"What's that?"

"You know," Ivy said, "the Lord's supper."

"Supper?" Maly asked, doubtful. "We have to be home at five."

"No, not supper like that. You eat at God's table. Then you're full of God and can come into His house."

"Oh, like going to a party?"

"Do you really have to drink blood?" Dicky asked suddenly.

"No," Ivy answered, "but I will when I grow up." He turned all the way around, slid down and sat on the bottom step under the altar just on the other side of the gate from Dicky. "And when you're grown up, you can, too."

"I'm going to build houses. Maybe I'll even build churches." Dicky's voice was a little more confident, and he rested back on his haunches.

"Okay," Maly said. "I'll make the Lord's supper, and then we have to go home."

She skipped down into the choir stalls, readjusting the magnolia leaf which had begun to slip. She took hymnals for dinner plates, prayer books for dessert, and white paper programs for napkins. When she came back to the communion railing, she had four place settings. "One for Dicky," she said, putting a hymnal, a prayer book and a program down before him, "and one for Ivy." She set Ivy's place where she had been kneeling. "And one for me." She was to sit in the center of the aisle, a step below them. Then she opened the gate, walked up to the altar and set a place beneath the cross, "And one for God."

Ivy hesitated, about to protest.

"She doesn't understand," Dicky explained.

"I do so. It's my turn. This is my game."

Dicky shrugged, unfolded his program and tucked it dutifully into his belt. Ivy held the gate open for Maly, then followed her out, and sat down to the dinner she had set for him. Maly crossed her legs and sank, Indian fashion, into the aisle.

She looked up at the two boys, Ivy in a light that made his hair almost blond, Dicky in a shadow that dulled his crew cut to rust. Perhaps, after all, they should be almost the same color. If she was going to be in the picture, she'd have to draw herself in.

Brother
and Sister

"My father is bigger than your father," the sister said.

The brother looked to middle space, vaguely enraged, his eleventh shot of vodka on an octagonal table the size of a dinner plate, set next to the large chair he was occupying. It occurred to him that this might be his sister's chair, though she was sitting across from him in something very upright and insubstantial.

"My chair is bigger than your chair," he tried, not convinced he had the hang of whatever game she was playing.

She took a sip of coca cola from a bottle and put it down on a carved chest, pimpled with coasters, small ash trays, lighters and painted stones. He took the same sort of sip from his shot glass, lips embracing it; and, when he had swallowed, he left the glass in his mouth and stuck his tongue out into it. She did not look at him, leaving him to enjoy himself or not. The light was very bright beyond her. He could neither hold the pose nor watch her for long; so he took the glass out, leaned over the arm of the chair and very carefully dropped the glass to the floor, watching as if rings might form and travel over the carpet. She turned at the sound, got up, picked up the glass and walked out of the room.

Having scored, he dozed for a moment, then woke generous with victory, if a little confused about it. They ought to go fishing. They always had a good time fishing. She didn't ever fish. She carried the lunch and sat on various rocks and didn't say anything at all. He admired himself in her eyes when she was like that. He cast and could see himself casting, a big man with a beautiful, accurate wrist.

"Are we going fishing some time?" he called out, but there was a machine on somewhere. "It's like a goddamned factory," he said and tried getting up to complain.

He didn't have trouble walking, for all the threat of little objects. Not exactly a cluttered room, just unexpected things, like that dinner plate table and those painted rocks. There was one of them in front of him now, probably a door stopper got loose from somewhere, traveling around the house on its own like a turtle. He'd have to be careful until he learned his way around, knew what he might meet, in light or dark.

By the time he found the kitchen, he had forgotten his negative intent. There was the vodka bottle for one thing and his sister for the other, standing with her back to him, staring at whatever she was grinding up in the sink. He leaned against the refrigerator, had a long blink, deciding against either fart or belch, opened his eyes and yawned instead. Somewhere in in the middle of it, she snapped a switch. The silence quite sobered him.

"I'm getting drunk," he said. The statement did not require an answer, and he got none; so he went to the bottle and helped himself. "Good and drunk."

"I'll feed you in a few minutes."

"Sounds like the zoo," he said. "Feeding time at the

26

zoo. You know, you've got to watch those turtles. They can be a real hazard to traffic around here. Guy could break his damned leg on one of them."

She had gone to the stove. Women's backs always looked offended, clothed or not. Never could see the erotic in a woman's back. Always offended.

"It's a nice place," he said. "I like it. I'm not mad about the turtles, I admit, but that's a matter of taste."

"And the snakes and the flying paper clips and the owl with elephantiasis," she said agreeably. "It gets crowded."

"Well, we're big people, with big imaginations," he said. "Some things you learn to put up with."

"I suppose."

"We've got the same father," he said then, testing.

"Maybe."

"Only I belittle him and you believe in him. There's no genetic argument. Our mother is a virtuous woman, in that narrow sense. Wouldn't you say so?"

"I'd say so."

"Good. Now, when are we going fishing?"

"Fishing?"

"Never mind," he said. "As long as we agree."

"You have to eat and then sleep a while. There are all these people coming in tonight."

"People?" There was something menacingly bland about her face as she turned to him. "Baby, what do we need with people? I've got all these lousy stories to tell you, and we can fight about all our relatives and talk about our post-Freudian childhood." Her expression hadn't changed. "Well, sure, people. Why not? We'll go fishing some other time. Another trip. Or come on up to Alaska with me now, why not?"

She was saying no in an elaborately long sentence, maybe more than one. He lost control of other people's speech long before he lost control of his own. And then she was talking about people, back at the stove again. He yawned once more until the tears came, but his head didn't quite clear. He got the people and the mushrooms in the pan connected, walked over and had a good look.

"This one's with Fink Brothers?" he asked for verification. "And what did you say to remember? The wife's mother is. . .?"

"A trustee."

"Some people have all the bad luck. You'd better feed me."

She did not wake him. A sharp, brief pain, as specifically located as a crack in the ice, brought him down into the sound of people in another room. He felt disagreeable but required. She had unpacked his suitcase, which was nice of her, though it made the whole process of dressing very difficult. Seeing his suit in the strange closet was no more friendly an experience than finding his face in the mirror, in living color without knobs to adjust. "And this is my Uncle Bill. . . by marriage. Poor, old Aunt Sarah." She couldn't get away with that. They were blood kin all right, past the blood in his eyes and his neck, nerve and bone kin. Bitch! bitched. "I am bigger than your father," he tried, and that cheered him up for a moment because the suit was the right size, and except for that face — too bad he couldn't unscrew it and replace it with an extra from his suitcase, something freshly cleaned and not too wrinkled — he was grossly impressive.

Perhaps he could get to a drink before he had to encounter anyone. He had stupidly given her all the liquor he'd brought with him. He tried to remember the geography of the house, a big house for someone who mostly lived alone. He might get down and out the front door, then around to the back and into the kitchen, but it was unlikely. He looked at his watch. It was eleven o'clock. Had she hoped finally he would not wake up? Easier the embarrassment of his absence than his presence? She wasn't like that. She didn't care. His sister.

In gold, a lighter shade but the same color as her Greek honey hair, which was a lighter shade but the same color as her Greek honey eyes. The man she was talking to looked beyond her through thick lenses and said something out of the side of his mouth, an animated cartoon.

"Mr. Magoo, come to life," the brother said, approaching the offered hand with what he considered to be a gentle smile.

The hand his sister tried to lay on him he took and kept for the whole circle of the room, as if instead they were children crossing a wide street. He wanted to look protective, though both of them knew that she was the one who wasn't afraid of dogs or cars. The room was full of both, women with low, barking voices, men peering through the windshields of their executive wooden frames, heavy and black this season.

"Alaska, yes," he said, and adjusted his ear to the floor trying to pick out the female noise far below him. It was easier to keep talking. "Yes, about our father's business — that vast, vulgar, meritricious what's-it."

She pulled him along.

"I'm having trouble with my contacts," he said, bare and bleeding-eyed, but more comfortable at their nearly mutual altitude, which gave them a sort of privacy wherever they were. "Shall I have a drink?"

"Why not?" she said.

There was a puppet behind the bar, a ridge of plastic hair painted black, eyes that closed when his head went too far back, voice of a queer batman in a World War Two movie. "Yes sir."

"No sir," the brother said, no human help there, and he wanted to accuse his sister as he prepared to abuse himself.

"Who's the crow-footed adolescent?" he asked

"That's the mother. . ."

"Trustee," he said, but of what he couldn't think.

He could not tell whether he had cast her off or had been cast off. He made his slow, enormous way across the room and sat down on the floor at the trustee's feet, watching first her shoes, then the controlled varicose veins in her legs, the boney awning of her lap, and skipped, in a failure of courage, to the crow's feet of her face. What was it he was supposed to remember? Had he been warned or required or simply entertained by details? Her flattered mouth, lipstick travelling up away from it in fine lines, smiled at him. He blinked for relief and then smiled back.

"We're both victims of the red spider," he said, knowing he must resist any temptation to explain, but of course she asked him. "An African god who sold his mother-in-law and children to Sky for just a couple of bits of technical information. You know, mother-in-law jokes aren't really funny. For example:. . ."

She did not laugh at the end of it, dutifully.

"But there's a real joke about a son-in-law," he said. "Which one *is* your son-in-law?"

She nodded across to Mr. Magoo, his mouth drawn in fast square and round shapes, slipping from side to side in his face.

"Ah, Mr. Magoo," he said and he didn't notice, studying his new subject, that she had stopped listening to him and was engaged instead, on her own level, with a younger, harder version of herself.

30

"I have not made a good impression," he said to her varicose veins, got up and went back to the bar.

Several men had gathered there and opened their conversation to him at once with a deference that came from respect for his size or his relative or both. He was feeling better, more affable, as if he had somehow followed instructions to the end of them and was now free.

"Don't know a goddamned thing about refrigeration plants or television or placer mining," he said. "One thing, and only one thing. . ." dramatic pause while he tried to and did remember what it was, "I'm a guy who knows how many beans it takes to make five."

How long she'd been standing by him he didn't know. When he saw her, he handed her his glass. Turning back to his audience, he found they were gone. She was, too, and he was alone by the bar, waiting for the puppet who was in no hurry to give him another drink.

Then he could not find all those people, the crow-footed adolescent, Mr. Magoo; they seemed to have gone somewhere in the house that he didn't know. He started down to the basement, but it was dark and quiet there. In the hall again, he could hear his sister's voice, a calling voice, and he went to find her at the open front door, a hand raised to the last guest on his way down the path.

"What the hell time is it?" he asked.

"Two-thirty," she said, walking past him to the kitchen where the puppet waited in a change of costume, his palm held up and out by an invisible string.

He went to where the bar had been and found it gone as well. It was unnerving.

"Sister!" he called. "Sister!" There she was, honey-colored still. "Christ! I thought maybe your stage had turned into a pumpkin, too. Is this whole place portable? Where can I get a drink?"

"In Alaska," she said.

"I'm not going to Alaska," he said.

"Aren't you?"

"No!" he shouted. "And you know goddamned well I'm not. I'm going to bed. Get me a drink."

She didn't hesitate so much as pause with that same bland danger in her face. "Mr. Magoo has the impression that you drink too much."

"A very perceptive fellow," the brother said generously. "Sounds like a prospective employer."

"He was."

"I thought you had a job."

"I do."

"Baby, get me a drink, and then I'll listen to all your troubles."

"When am I going to listen to yours?"

"Any time," he said. "Any time at all. Let me tell you about this WCTU sister I've got, for one thing."

But once she had given him the bottle of vodka, he became aware of the effect of his badly interrupted sleep.

"These parties in the middle of the night... I don't see how you take it."

He always woke very early. He was glad to see a last drink in the bottle. He took it carefully, not to shock his gut into revolt, and then waited to measure the little good it would do. There was something unpleasant, like disappointment, just below the pain in his head, which was sending its own messages. There had been some sort of party that he'd got out of bed for. Had his sister been unhappy about something? It was none of his business, a head full of griefs of his own which he had trouble enough keeping there out of her way. Alaska: "and he came out of the jungle rich, rich. . ." or whatever the hell it was. Was it today he had said he was going to Alaska? On the afternoon plane, that was it. The trouble was, you loved what you were related to. Accepting that, he tried to stay in bed a while, knowing she would get up as soon as she heard him; but a horizontal hangover wasn't to be endured for more than moments at a time. Once he was on his feet, he kept encountering objects. Wasn't that the chest of drawers from their grandmother's house? He thumbed the corner which had just bruised his side, knowing it for the corner that had scarred his head, at the hairline, during a game of blind man's buff. He had not known he was hurt until he heard her crying. After having considered and discarded various means of revenge, he went into the bathroom for a shower.

She knew about his breakfast: a glass of milk and a glass of orange juice with an egg in it; and he knew about her breakfast: silence with whatever else she decided on. A quiet woman anyway except with machines and pots and pans. Odd that she didn't marry, really, being so quiet, being the color of good whiskey or honey, all that color in the summer, carrying the memory of it in her eyes and hair on winter mornings like this one. She had her bad points. Quietness. In a conversation, what she had to say were just pieces broken off her silence, hard clues to it. You had to know her to know her. Sometimes he did. Sometimes he didn't. She might be irritated or sorry or nothing at all right now. That was unpleasant, disappointing. He looked at his watch to be sure an hour had passed since his first drink. He stood in the kitchen for his second.

"We could walk for an hour before you have to go," she said.

There was a hill to climb, a path that began wide enough for two to walk together, then narrowed for the first steep pitch, and, even though she knew the way, he went ahead because he always did, and he chose the place to stop as well, giving her breath as a gift from him. It was beginning to feel that way now. They climbed again, then stopped again, and then he went on alone, up toward the sky he had been sold to, which was not far away. At the top of the hill he looked back to see himself being seen by her, and she was there watching him, a big man against a near sky.

"I am bigger than your father," he called to her, grateful.

But when he climbed back down to her, he saw that she was crying, and then he had to know how badly hurt he was, just for that moment, and to forgive her for it.

House

"It's a case of retarded development," Harry shouted. "You're thirty years old."

Anna, kneeling on the floor by a half reupholstered couch, looked up at him and smiled through a mouth full of tacks. Then she went back to her hammering, letting it punctuate or machine gun down his complaints, depending on their accuracy.

"Other women *want* to buy houses. Other women *want* their kids to have a yard to play in. They like to reupholster their *own* furniture. They don't have to be *dragged*, screaming and kicking, into middle class and middle age. They take *pleasure* in it."

Anna's answer was fortunately both short and incomprehensible though it was not difficult for Harry to imagine what of his army vocabulary she was returning to him. Other women not only didn't say that sort of thing; they didn't let their husbands get away with it either. But lecturing her about that would be side-tracking the argument. The first step toward civilization had to be taken before the subtleties could be considered.

"Wouldn't you just look?" he asked, trying to sound more reasonable. "Just drive around with the kids this afternoon and look?"

She pounded in the last of her mouthful of tacks. "Harry, baby," she said, "I've told you what I'm doing with *my* money. Six more months of chewing tacks, and I'm buying that island."

"I'll sell the boat," he said. "I will. I'll sell it. It was ridiculous to buy it in the first place. *Your* money! What about *my* money?"

"So buy a house," she said.

"I haven't got the money. You know perfectly well I haven't. Anyway, it's supposed to be for you. You're supposed to want it."

"I know," she said. "I'm depriving the kids. Now they play in two hundred acres of public park, thirty miles of beach, and spend their week-ends cooped up in a boat, when instead they could have a thirty foot wide back yard and a wading pool. And you could mow the lawn and I could overstuff our own furniture. You know what I think, Harry. I think the only thing between you and being an overstuffed shirt is me, and I'm getting bored with it. An island's just right. Sell the boat; buy yourself a house. When you miss us, swim over."

"My kids are not living on any island. . ."

"That's telling her, Harry," Joey said, wandering in from the kitchen with a banana, shoeless and shirtless, his very small jeans riding low.

"Don't call me Harry!"

"Who is this guy, Mom?" Joey asked, jerking his head toward his father. "I thought his name was Harry."

"Oh, he's some sort of real estate agent." Anna said.

"He is not," Doll bellowed, an even smaller version of

her brother, identically dressed with a similar banana. "He's my father."

"Doll, honey," Harry said, "Joey? Don't you guys think it would be fun to live in a house, I mean a real house with trees around it and grass and rooms of your own?"

"Sure," Doll said, "if I can sleep in Joey's room."

"You don't want to live out on an island, do you? Summer time's all right, but what would you do in the winter time? Where would you go to school?"

"With the fish?" Joey suggested and then fell onto the open springs of the couch in delight at his own joke.

"I'm not kidding," Harry said, a hurt in his voice that alerted and sobered them all. "I really think it's time we all grew up."

"You are grown up," Doll protested.

"How much older than six do you have to be?" Joey asked.

"You don't have to be any older," Harry said, "than how much older than six you are."

"And a half," Joey said, thoughtfully.

"Come on," Anna said. "Find your shoes, mine too, while you're at it. Dad wants to go for a drive."

"Why do we need shoes?" Doll asked.

Anna nodded to Harry for explanation. He could think of nothing but a stern look which amused both children into obedience.

It was no good, on a beautiful summer Saturday, to come out of their shabby apartment block, get into their car and turn away from beach, yacht club and park to drive into the residential sections of the city, rows of stucco bungalows with high basements on thirty foot lots. Though Harry knew these flat lands were where they should begin, the way the rest of their friends had ten years ago, he drove through them to the city hills where lots were fifty or sixty, sometimes even one hundred feet wide, where houses were set high on the land to look out over bay and mountains, the same view they already had from their kitchen and the condemned balcony beyond it. It had been a great view when everyone else they knew lived in ugly, little closed-in houses, but now their friends were moving up onto these hills, enjoying the view from large, well furnished living rooms, from terraces with garden furniture. Nobody else he knew had a cabin cruiser, but some people were buying outboard motors. Who needed to sleep out on the water on a Saturday night if he had a house like one of these to come home to?

"The McLeans have just bought that place," Harry said, slowing so that everyone could see enough to share his envy. "There's a fish pond beyond that hedge, with gold fish in it."

The children sounded dutifully interested in the gold fish. Anna said nothing. They drove on, passing occasionally a house for sale, some marked "open house", but they were expensive, even pretentious places, and anyway the kids weren't properly dressed, nor was Anna, in work trousers, sneakers, and an old shirt of his. Then Joey threw one of Doll's shoes out of the window, and Harry had to stop the car, get out and go back for it. Walking back, he looked at the car, the same one he'd had when they got married, a great car then, a souped up Buick with all the paint burned off it, full now of sulking wife and fighting kids. A man, pushing a new power mower, looked up with detached interest.

"Shoe," Harry said, holding up what even the Good Will would not have taken. There was really nothing for the man to answer. "Well, forget it," Harry said, getting into the car and slamming the door. Once he could have cut out with blasted mufflers. Now the car could only cough like a rest home patient and moan up the rest of the hill.

"Out sight-seeing or house hunting on Saturday?" McLean asked Harry as they took a break from checking specifications for a new school.

"Just out on a drive," Harry said.

"Something wrong with the boat?"

"No. As a matter of fact, I'm thinking of selling it."

"No kidding?"

"Well, you know, it can get to be like everything else."

"It's a honey of a boat."

"Yeah," Harry said, but he didn't get any pleasure from the admiration, perhaps because it was no longer tinged with envy as it used to be.

Oh, Harry had been the lucky one, all right, the cake-and-eat-it-too boy. His wife liked noisy cars and boats and crazy apartments. She also liked beer parlors and foot ball games. So did all the other girls, until about two weeks after they were married. Then suddenly it was Austins and mortgages and t.v. sets. But not for Anna. She couldn't have cared less. That is, she did care. "If you're going to watch the fights, watch the fights," she'd say, and so they left their friends to the eye strain of the five dollar down, five dollar a month flickering screens and went to the fights, the meets, the games: ring side, fifty yard line living. And Harry and Anna were the only ones who didn't have a child anywhere from six months to a year after they were married. Joey took a lovely, leisurely three and a half years to turn up. By that time they had the boat. Harry knew perfectly well that the boat was all that kept them in touch with most of the crowd, and even the boat didn't change the wives' attitude toward Anna. It would have been all right if Anna had been just one of those buddy kinds of women, trying to outswim, outrun, or outyell any man she was with. She did sometimes try that, of course, but never with anything but fun in it, fun finally to catch up with her, tumble her into the drink and go after her again. She looked better in a bathing suit than other women could take. The baby was supposed to change all that. Harry's friends warned him with malice and sympathy. And Harry half believed them. He even tried to get ready for it, thinking of mortgaging the boat to get a down payment for a house, but Anna never mentioned a house. She talked about going to Europe instead. And three months after Joey was born, that's what they did because he was not much more trouble then than a back pack. It was a marvelous summer, Joey their human passport in every village.

"Listen, McLean, a kid's a social asset if you've got the right attitude about it," Harry explained when they got back.

The salary he'd given up and the money they'd spent worried Anna not at all. She decided to start reupholstering furniture. Space? Their living room. They'd never got round to buying much besides beds. So what she worked on during the day, they sat on in the evening, and she made money at it.

Harry had always wondered a little more than Anna how other people lived. He had what she called "patches of worry" about things. For instance, because the kids slept in what should have been the dining room, they never had people over for dinner. They entertained on the boat or in Chinatown or at the Greek Village. And they didn't watch television. The kids seemed more interested in clam digging or tree climbing than in anything that kept them indoors, and Harry and Anna read a lot, sitting in the comfortable corners of other people's furniture.

"They call me the Frenchman at the office because I

40

never entertain at home," Harry would say, or "Television has its good points, after all."

What weighed on his mind most of all was their lack of debt and Anna's savings account. In a good mood, he'd explain he had nothing to gripe about at coffee breaks, no killing mortgages, no idle, money spending wife. In a bad mood, he brooded about what they must be doing to the economy of the country, which survived and grew, as far as he could tell, on interest payments.

"Let's buy a plane then," Anna would say. "We could have some race horses."

It took Harry two weeks after that first drive into lawndom to raise the subject again, this time beginning more casually and quietly.

"McLean's started fuchsia cuttings in his office window."

"You could take one of your avacado pits down," Anna suggested.

"For his garden," Harry said.

"You want to be a gardener? Hire yourself out on Saturdays, two dollars an hour."

"Anna, couldn't you be happy in a house? Couldn't we just try?"

"You mean for psychological interest? We could hire ourselves out for the air-raid shelter project. They pay the whole family."

"But we know about that, honey. What I want to know is, can't we live with space?"

"That's a pretty exclusive project," Anna said. "I don't think we're the right material."

"I am being serious," Harry shouted. "I am asking you, as my wife, if you could live in a house, H O U S E."

"Why?"

"Because I would like to do something *ordinary*, for a

41

change. I am an ordinary man, and I'd like to be ordinary just to see what it's like."

"Kids!" Anna shouted. "Shoes. We're going house hunting."

"And not just shoes this time," Harry said. "House hunting and beach combing have different costumes. We've got to look well turned out."

"Then we've got to go shopping first," Anna said.

"I will not be distracted."

"You are distracted," Anna said. "You're out of your mind."

But that was her last negative comment. Saturdays and Sundays for six weeks the boat stayed tied up at the dock while Harry, Anna, Joey and Doll became experts on open houses and empty houses, everything for sale from the bottom of the hills to the top. The kids, reluctant at first, adapted and developed skills for this new game. Joey, in a number phase, memorized down payments and mortgage rates. Doll became obsessive about colored plumbing. Harry catalogued views and fruit trees. Anna spent most of her time in basements. At the end of each hunting day, they would vote on the house they all liked best. It was never unanimous. Some days they had to settle on any house that had the approval of only two of them. Then Joey would give them the figures, Doll the state of the plumbing, and Anna the cost of rewiring or new hot water tank or copper piping or furnace. The result was always the same. Unless they sold the boat, they couldn't afford anything they were looking at.

"Well, why not?" Harry asked finally. "Why not sell it?"

"And just always house hunt on Saturdays and Sundays?" Joey asked.

"Watch television," Doll said.

"If we sold the boat, we could buy a television," Harry said.

"Why don't we take next week-end off and go out on the boat?" Anna suggested.

"As a sort of farewell?"

Harry couldn't have had better luck with the weather. It rained. He couldn't have had better luck with the boat either. Everything in it had gone cranky with neglect, including the people, who had forgotten how to live pleasantly at such close quarters.

"It smells," Joey said.

"It squeaks," Doll said.

"It needs money spent on it," Anna said.

"That settles it," Harry said.

And it seemed to. Anna, Joey, and Doll climbed off the boat on Sunday night without so much as a regretful look backward. It was Harry who stood for a reluctant moment in the rain with all those sunny memories. Anna put the ad in the paper. And Anna showed the strangers over the boat. The night Harry was supposed to sign the papers, he became generous with hesitations.

"If this seems selfish to you, honey," he said, "I'm perfectly willing to talk about it."

"Sign," Anna said.

After that, they had to buy a house. There was no reason not to. And they found one, not quite up on the hill but tilting in that direction, and there was a view of the mountains if you left the frosted window open in the upstairs bathroom, which had a violet toilet and yellow tub and basin. There were fruit trees and a dried up pond in the sixty foot yard. There was a television aerial on the roof. It had lots of rooms, not very big ones, but Joey figured out that there were two rooms apiece with two left over. The down payment was small enough and the mortgage big enough so that they had cash left over for a television and some furniture.

"Why don't we just go ahead and trade in the car?" Harry said, a note of panic in his voice.

"Why not?" Anna agreed.

"I mean, we could get a new little Austin. . ."

And they did, a grey one. Joey said it smelled funny. Doll said it squeaked, but Anna pointed out that it didn't need any money spent on it, that is, except for the monthly payments.

The night before they moved, Harry lay on his back staring up at the familiar foot steps over his head. That morning McLean had said, "I never thought I'd see the day when you looked like a candidate for ulcers. What's the matter with you?"

"Bills," Harry had said and said it again now.

"What?" Anna said.

"Honey, are we making a terrible mistake?"

"Sure," Anna said. "That's the way we like to live."

"But this is different."

"What's different about it?"

"The boat, for instance. Now, if that was a mistake, it was our own. This is the sort of mistake everybody makes."

"Right," Anna said. "Ordinary."

And that's all she would say. She went to sleep, leaving him with that terrible and lonely idea, which had been his idea all along.

The next night was worse because there they all were, exhausted from the move, baffled by the new furniture and all the rooms.

"I think I'm deaf," Joey said, as he was getting into bed. "I can't hear anybody anywhere."

And Doll had to come down the stairs to tell them she was crying. It obviously seemed to her a very odd message to deliver, but she was grown up about it. They moved her bed into Joey's room. It had to go up against the closet door until they could figure out a better way to arrange the furniture. The old dining room had been bigger, or maybe it simply hadn't had any closet doors to get in the way.

On his back that night, Harry didn't have the courage to say what a terrible mistake it all was. He fell asleep wanting to cry and dreamed all that had happened to them, lost in furniture stores, in vaults of banks, the boat sinking under them with mortgages floating about in the debris.

In the morning he could hardly get out of bed, yet he wanted to get out, right out, get into his car. Then he remembered the Austin, and his sense of disgust was physical.

"Maybe I've got the 'flu," he said.

"No, you haven't," Anna said. "You just haven't got your land legs yet. Stand up."

The kids were cheerful enough after they found their way downstairs, but, when Joey turned on the television before they sat down to breakfast, Anna's swat lifted him right across the room. Breakfast was very tentative and mannerly in the dining room.

"Sort of like an English boarding house, isn't it?" Anna said. "I should cool the toast in the kitchen."

All day at the office Harry swung from daring plans for escape to depressing hopes that they might all get used to it. At dead center between these two solutions was his conviction that he just didn't have the kind of courage it took to be all these good things: a middle class, middle aged man with a mortgage and an Austin. And sooner or later, Anna was going to face him with it. Why hadn't they bought that crazy island? Or a plane or a race horse? Something to feel guilty and defensive and proud about. What could you feel about a house, particularly an ordinary, sensible sort of house with a dried up pond in the back yard? You could feel awful, and that's what Harry felt, bobbing along in the smelly, squeaky, little Austin, eighteen months off even being his own, toward a house he'd be paying for for fifteen years.

On the front porch, he thought the noise must be coming from somewhere else, but in the front hall, the heavy thuds and falling plaster were clearly his concern. He lept up the stairs, calling as he went, opened the door to Doll's room, empty now but for a chest of drawers, just in time to see a wrecking bar break through another patch of wall.

"What are you doing?" he shouted, peering at Anna through the ragged hole. Behind her on Joey's bed, the two children sat, their attention as fixed as it might have been on television. "What the devil are you doing?"

"We decided there were too many rooms," Anna said.

"But how do you know that's not a supporting wall?"

"I don't," she said. "It may be a mistake," and she let the wrecking bar crash through the wall again. "On the other hand, it may be a solution. Here, take a turn. You'll like it."

He stood with the wrecking bar in his hand, doubtful. Then he swung it at the wall and felt the plaster give. Over the sound of falling bits, he heard the kids cheering.

"That's great," he said, and he did it again.

"So we can get rid of the dining room," Anna said, "and we can bash our way through to a view. And we can tear down the back porch."

"Marvelous," he said and swung again.

"We're going to put a ladder up to the back door," Joey shouted.

"And sit on the toilet and look at the view," Doll explained.

46

"I sent back the t.v.," Anna said.

"Lovely," he said, and he knew, in his delight, that they might go too far, might tear down the whole place by mistake, but that didn't matter. After all, it was theirs, mortgage and all. The house rang with the wrecking bar again.

"Easy now," Anna said. "Easy, baby. I'm not quite ready for outer space."

"But you could be," Harry said, "if we ever decided to move."

A
Television Drama

At one-thirty in the afternoon, Carolee Mitchell was running the vacuum cleaner, or she would have heard the first sirens and looked out. After the first, there weren't any others. The calling voices, even the number of dogs barking, could have been students on their way back to school, high spirited in the bright, cold earliness of the year. Thinking back on the sounds, Carolee remembered a number of car doors being slammed, that swallow of air and report which made her smooth her hair automatically even if she wasn't expecting anyone. But what caught her eye finally was what always caught her eye. the flight of a bird from a tree top in the ravine out over the fringe of trees at the bottom of her steeply sloping front lawn, nearly private in the summer, exposed now to the startling activity of the street.

Three police cars were parked in front of the house, a motorcycle like a slanted stress in the middle of the inter-section, half a dozen more police cars scattered up and down the two blocks. There were men in uniform up on her neighbor's terrace with rifles and field glasses. Police with dogs were crossing the empty field at the bottom of the ravine. More cars were arriving, police and reporters with cameras and sound equipment. Mingling among the uniforms and equipment were the neighbors: Mrs. Rolston from the house across the street who had obviously not taken time to put on a coat and was rubbing her arms absent-mindedly as she stood and talked, Jane Carey from next door with a scarf tied round her head and what looked like one of her son's jackets thrown over her shoulders, old Mr. Monkson, a few small children. Cars and people kept arriving. Suddenly there was a voice magnified to reach even Carolee, surprised and unbelieving behind her picture window.

"Clear the street. All householders return to or stay in your houses. Clear the street."

Mrs. Rolston considered the idea for a moment but did not go in. The others paid no attention at all. Carolee wondered if she should go out just to find out what on earth was going on. Perhaps she should telephone someone, but everyone she might phone was already in the street. Was it a gas main? Not with all those dogs. A murder? It seemed unlikely that anyone would kill anyone else on this street, where every child had his own bedroom and most men either studies or basement workshops to retreat into. In any case, it was the middle of the afternoon. Mrs. Cole had come out on her balcony with field glasses focused on the place where the dogs and police had entered the ravine. Field glasses. Where were Pete's field glasses? Carolee thought she knew, but she did not move to get them. She would not know what she was looking for in the undergrowth or the gardens.

"Clear the street. All householders return to or stay in your houses."

Police radios were now competing with each other. "Suspect last apprehended in the alley between. . ." "House to house search. . ." "Ambulance. . ."

If one of those policemen standing about on the street would come to search the house, Carolee could at least find out what was going on. Was that a t.v. crew? Dogs were barking in the ravine. Did police dogs bark? Nobody on the street seemed to be doing anything, except for the motor-cycle policeman who was turning away some cars. Maybe Carolee should go empty the dishwasher and then come back. It was pointless to stand here by the window. Nothing was happening, or, if something was happening, Carolee couldn't see the point of it. She went to the window in Pete's study to see if she could discover activity on the side street. There were more policemen, and far up the block an ambulance was pulling away without a siren, its red light slowly circling. Carolee watched it until it turned the corner at the top of the hill. Then she turned back toward the sound of barking dogs and radios, but paused as she turned.

There, sitting against the curve of the laurel hedge by the lily pond, was a man, quite a young man, his head down, his left hand against his right shoulder. He was sick or hurt or dead. Or not really there at all, something Carolee's imagina-tion had put there to explain the activity in the street, part of a collage, like an unlikely photograph in the middle of a painting. But he raised his head slightly then, and Carolee saw the blood on his jacket and trousers.

"I must call the police," she said aloud, but how could she call the police when they were already there, three of them standing not seventy feet away, just below the trees on the parking strip? She must call someone, but all the neighbors were still out of doors. And what if the police did discover him? He might be shot instead of helped. Carolee wanted to help him, whoever he was. It was such an odd way he was sitting, his legs stretched out in front of him so that he couldn't possibly have moved quickly. He might not be able to move at all. But she couldn't get to him, not without being seen. Suddenly he got to his feet, his left hand still against his right shoulder and also holding the lower part of his ducked face. He walked to the end of the curve of hedge as if it was very difficult for him to move, and then he began a stumbling run across the front lawn, through the trees, and out onto the parking strip. There he turned, hesitated, and fell on his back. Carolee had heard no shot. Now her view was blocked by a gathering of police and reporters, drawn to that new center like leaves to a central drain.

"Suspect apprehended on. . ."

What had he done? What had that hurt and stumbling boy done? Carolee was standing with her hand on the transistor radio before it occurred to her to turn it on.

"We interrupt this program with a news bulletin. A suspect has been apprehended on. . ."

He had robbed a bank, run a car into a tree, shot a policeman, been shot at.

"And now, here is our reporter on the scene."

Carolee could see the reporter quite clearly, standing in the street in front of the house, but she could hear only the radio voice, explaining what had happened.

"And now the ambulance is arriving. . ." as indeed it was. "The suspect, suffering from at least three wounds, who seems near death, is being lifted onto a stretcher . . ." This she couldn't see. It seemed to take a very long time before police cleared a path for the ambulance, again silent, its red light circling, to move slowly down the block and out of sight.

A newspaper reporter was walking up the front path, but Carolee didn't answer the door. She stood quietly away from the window and waited until he was gone. Then she went to the kitchen and began to empty the dishwasher. It was two-o'clock. She turned on the radio again to listen to the regular news report. The details were the same. At three o'clock the hospital had reported that the policeman was in the operating room having a bullet removed from his right lung. At four o'clock the suspect was reported in only fair condition from wounds in the shoulder, jaw, leg and hand.

At five o'clock Pete came home, the evening paper in his hand. "Well, you've had quite a day," he said. "Are you all right?"

"Yes," Carolee said, her hands against his cold jacket, her cheek against his cold face. "Yes, I'm all right. What did the paper say?"

"It's all diagrams," he said, holding out the front page to her.

There was a map of the whole neighborhood, a sketched aerial map, a view of the roof of their house Carolee had never had. She followed the dots and arrows to the hood of a car crumpled under a flower of foliage, on again across the ravine, up their side hill, and there was the laurel hedge and the jelly bean lily pond, but the dots didn't stop there, arced round rather and immediately down through the trees to a fallen doll, all alone, not a policeman or reporter in sight, lying there exposed to nothing but a God's eye view.

"You must have seen him," Pete said.

"Yes," Carolee agreed, still looking down on the roof tops of all her neighbors' houses.

"Did it frighten you?" Pete asked.

"Not exaclty. It was hard to believe, and everything seemed to happen so very slowly."

"Did you get a good look at him?"

"I guess not really," Carolee said. Had he sat there by the laurel hedge at all, his long, stiff legs stretched out in front of him? The map didn't show it.

"Something has got to be done about all this violence," Pete said.

His tone and the look on his face made Carolee realize that Pete had been frightened, much more frightened than she was. Those dotted lines across his front lawn, that figure alone in the landscape — Carolee felt herself shaken by a new fear, looking at what Pete had seen.

"I'll get us a drink," Pete said.

Once they sat down, Carolee tried to tell her husband what it had been like, all those women just standing out in the street. She told him about the guns and field glasses and dogs and cameras. She did not tell him about the man, hurt, by the laurel hedge.

Pete turned on the television, and they watched three minutes of fast moving images, first the policeman lifted into an ambulance, then officers and dogs running through the field, finally glimpses of the suspect on the ground and then shifted onto a stretcher; and, while they watched, a voice told them of the robbery, the chase, the capture. Finally several people were quickly interviewed, saying such things as, "I saw him go over the fence" or "He fell practically at my feet." That was Mrs. Rolston, still rubbing her cold arms in the winter day.

"I'm glad you had the good sense to stay inside," Pete said. He was holding her hand, beginning to relax into indignation and relief.

Carolee wasn't there, nor was the man there. If she had spoken to that reporter, if she had said then, "I saw him. He was sitting by the laurel hedge," would the dots in the paper have changed? Would the cameras have climbed into their nearly exposed winter garden? Would she believe now what she couldn't quite believe even then, that she stood at that window and saw a man dying in her garden?

Now a labor union boss was talking, explaining the unfair practices of the compensation board. Nearly at once, young marines were running, firing, falling. Planes were dropping bombs. Carolee wasn't there, but it seemed real to her, terribly real, so that for a moment she forgot Pete's hand in hers, her safe house on a safe street, and was afraid.

Theme for Diverse Instruments

Although she has cared about sources, traced herself back to the Daughters of the American Revolution, the Colonial Dames, back to admirals, generals and presidents, back farther still across an ocean to a valley of giants, of free men greater than kings, importantly she herself is the source, the Amazonian mother of us all, whose personal history is the text of our inheritance and of our faith. And, if we were born to outlive and even to outgrow her, we can still never be certain that the shadows we cast are not her own. Her delusions of grandeur become our reality.

A picture of her, postcard to the world, standing in the vaulted hollow of a redwood tree, arms outstretched commanding attention. Halt! I am the measure of creation! by which we shall know the tree and the blade of grass. That's a pretty big tree. And she's ridiculous, isn't she, standing there in her Queen Mary clothes, a piece of jewelery hung around her neck like a royal honor or a trophy? Hands in white gloves, like Jim Crow in a minstrel show, but white faced, too, in the dark womb of that tree, her real, her androgynous parent. It is a very big tree, if you'll remember that she's six feet tall with a wing spread that hasn't been measured. And whichever one of us — there are a number of generations now — took that picture is taller than she, taking her as a measure, and we all do, and we all are taller than she, having her to thank for it. But we didn't begin that way.

She does not speak of the births of all her children, only the birth of the twins, two pains, one for each, and she could have had them alone in the woods, only it would have taken a little longer. Perhaps that's what she's really doing in this picture, standing between her own miraculous thighs with a fisherman's gesture, and they *were* big, too, one seven-and-a-half and one nine-and-a-half pounds. She herself weighed two hundred and eighty pounds before they were born. It took two strong men, the colored butler and the cook's boy friend, to get her up the stairs, but then she was on her own, and it was easy. Her youngest child, a girl, claimed to have miscarried twins. "Women in this family don't miscarry!" Take her, for example, and we all do. Mother of Amazons, a tribe in herself, her womb housing an army. Even the offspring of her daughters and her daughters-in-law became her children, and so have their children, generations of siblings to a common mother.

She has wanted us all to live, and we have, through childhood diseases, depressions, wars, and even her own tyranny. There have been a number of accidents but few perversions. People in this family don't . . . often. One of us stammered until she forbade it. Another held her breath until a hose knocked the wind back into her. One of us shat behind her chair, but only once. And two of us rode a pregnant sow to death, but that didn't do any good either. We have stolen and set fire to things and tried to kill each other. We have won prizes and awards and even medals. We have written poems for each other, operated on each other, given each other commissions in the army, forty percent discounts, used clothes, and some sympathy. She has wanted us all to live, and we have.

So has she: too mean to die before she can contest her brother-in-law's will, before she can legally give away all her money, before she can certify her oldest daughter for psychotic kindness; too curious to die before one son-in-law generals the whole country into action with his atomic pornography, before another defeats integration single-handed by taking a nigger to lunch, before still another wipes out an entire nation by refusing to learn Japanese; too proud to die before her youngest granddaughter marries a corporation to silence rumors of virgin birth, before her eldest great-grandson buys out Rockefeller's liberal interest with his paper route money, before at least one of her own is dead; too alive to die even after she's dead, in that backward action of second birth, in which the funeral cake becomes the communion, and we swallow her, hook, line, and sinker, to burst full grown again, some sort of transvirgin Athena, out of a redwood tree, which we call virgin timber, for all its phallic surprise.

Who in hell does she think she is, anyway? Our source, our Freudian mistake, our absolute female patriarch. Well, if you can't be human, there's only one other energetic choice, and she made it: she became an idea.

And to the next question — whose idea is she, anyway? — there is no simple answer, not even her own, though we'll have to settle down to that, too, eventually, if we're going to get anywhere. The problem is that our own point of view isn't simply reliable. This 'quarrelsome we' have already been involved in a number of discrepancies, irritations, and open arguments in just a few hundred words. We can't even always reach an agreement of subject and verb, for just there we falter between our common source and our singularities. Not even the twins are identical, the delivered or the miscarried. Some among us are convinced that 'we' is a front for only one of our number, young Arachne, a fouled up, paranoiac spider, ready to hang herself, if she's got to, for revenge. Others of us are inclined to believe that young Orestes is being pursued through these pages to some final sanctuary of forgiveness and the rule of law, the recovery of the true patriarch. But he, our literary critic, denies responsibility and claims the mild disturbance of syntax, the single entry of a four letter word (in the past tense), and the reference to myth are all group pretensions toward a middle class stream of consciousness, pretensions which one of our amateur sociologists would rather relate to the nouveau riche who advance from storing newspapers in bathtubs to planting vines in thunder mugs and lavabos. The only lawyer in the family assures us that, whatever the case is, we'll all sue.

But not until she's gone, and we're very reluctant to let her go, for all our angry theories about her own will power. This last illness is only one example, but it will do for now. The doctors were not sure whether it was the fall that made her break her hip or the broken hip that made her fall, a common confusion of cause and effect in the circular time of the aged, where nights are measured by slow, very slow, round trips to the toilet. Anyway, she lay there on the tile floor, as all of us fear we will sooner or later, frightened and enraged and embarrassed, a foot tangled in the laundry basket, a shoulder on the scales, cheek by jowl with the toilet bowl, the nearest thing she'd had to a bedfellow for years, back against the cold side of the tub, which failed by a foot and a half to measure her length, a child's coffin. Nobody, at first, wants to be found, not like that. But pain and cold and helplessness gradually limit dignity as well as a sense of humor. She called, and one of us heard, in the dream we have all had more than once, the imperious voice which is child and mate and mother to which there is no answer but yes. And, though she couldn't be moved until the ambulance men arrived, her oldest daughter had already tugged fiercely to pull the nightdress down over the old buttocks, had covered her more completely with a blanket, had sat there on the toilet bowl to hold her mother's hand and stroke her mother's hair.

The operation took place the next day, a pin set in that joint worn out by the eighty-three years of weight, her own and ours. And there she lay, pinned together again (it wasn't the first time) like a grotesque and beloved old doll, resurrected for yet another generation. But this time, for the first time, her heart was uncertain. It would not let her simply rest and recover. It galloped, bucked, stopped against the pain, started, stopped, started, in an endless and various tantrum which bladder, bowel, stomach, lungs, and finally brain must all contend with, until the organs of her body were all her enemies, pain her one, gentle, obscene familiar. And outside the cage of her body were the needles and voices of life, opening, sewing up, deadening, quickening, scolding, scoffing, scheming, screaming. She was screaming, God, screaming. We could hear her in the parking lot, in the waiting room, in the corridors, for hours and hours until a shot of morphine that could kill a horse would quiet the world to the chronic cough, uncertain moan, fretful cry of simple mortality.

The nurses were not resigned; they quit, unwilling but also unable to command or appease such a rage. We could have allowed them to kill it, the rage, the pain, and the heart, but we are not ordinary children of an ordinary mother. What she has never allowed us to forget, we could not allow her to forget now.

Every one of her immediate children came, and other generations sent representatives. Then we organized ourselves. Sister and brother coupled for each shift at the hospital, and behind those front lines were numbers of others to cook, to drive, to answer telephones and letters. One young historian spent a month making a rather curious scrap book of the campaign in which she could later find get-well cards, pressed flowers, birth announcements, photographs, newspaper clippings, kindergarten drawings, and other small manifestos of need for which she has been so long the recipient, the marvelous garbage can to which all our triumphs are destined.

She was not what you would call co-operative even then. She spat in the face of a son, bit a daughter, tried to strangle herself with the ribbons of her bedjacket, tried to get out of bed, and emptied her bowels against her restrainers. She screamed and screamed, accusing us all of inadequacies, infidelities, brutalities, plots against her death. We were, of course, guilty. Without us she could have died, but we have wanted her to live, and she has.

One morning at dawn, after several hours of struggling sleep, she opened her eyes and spoke in her natural voice to one of her twin sons and her youngest daughter.

"How long have you been here, children?"

All our life, mama, all our life. No one begrudged these two that particular moment, for they are the handsomest among us, the first son by twenty minutes, the last daughter by ten years. And they are the tallest, too, of the first generation. He is not the most successful, and she has threatened the family honor with mythical miscarriages and premature births, but, if our mother was to be lucid again, surely the morning light should rise on beauty to make her glad of her creation.

Arrogant, brutal, bloody nonsense! (the voice of that

British in-law? or Orestes back from a year at Oxford?) A circus side show, a family of pituitary freaks, suffering a gladular psychosis: we are the gentle giants to be literally looked up to, not at. Matricide is not one of our parlor tricks. Over mercy killing we choose unmerciful living, race of martyrs, race of sad clowns, Oedipal, anal, anxious, and proud.

She lives, reduced somewhat. About a hundred and fifty pounds actually. She doesn't walk at all any more, but even before the accident she didn't walk much, her spine ankylosed from severe arthritis thirty-five years ago. We have bought her a hospital bed, and the younger twin has built a derrick with a canvas swing by which she can be hoisted out of bed and lowered into her Danish invalid's chair, still hooked by a tube to her bottle of urine and to her television set by the remote control cord. She reads a little still, against the slowly growing cataracts, and she sews, making bedjackets, layettes, and padded coat hangers for us and for charity, the needle held by the flat pressure of thumb and straight first finger. She has not been able to make a fist of either hand for thirty-five years.

For company she has us and her nurses. We hang by families on all four walls, the only segregated generation the latest where the count is still important, a little population explosion all by itself between the bathroom door and the corner.

She can pay for the nurses herself now that she's mortally certain of winning her case against her dead brother-in-law. An agreement is an agreement, and he signed away his estate, some ten thousand dollars, when she agreed to pay him fifty dollars a month while he lived. He didn't live long, four sick years while another widowed sister-in-law nursed him. He tried to leave his money to her out of some senile sentimentality, simply forgetting his legal debt, which was moral, too, for our father had supported that brother most of his life, poor farmer, lay preacher, childless widower whose simple pleasure it was to take a lady friend flying on a Saturday afternoon. But the money now must go to the white uniformed derrick stewardesses, not for trips over Louisville and farm land and the wide Ohio River but instead over the exotic landscape of an oriental carpet one of us, the conqueror, brought home in 1945. She commutes daily over that tree of life from bed to chair and back again, a collapsing dirigible, swinging over the tree of life, moored there by television set and urine bottle. She's mortally certain she has her fare. It must be one of the reasons she lives. We can't be completely to blame.

"I was out of my mind there for a while," she says to each of us who comes to call, searching over her glasses for something more than acceptance, something less than forgiveness. Then to her gentle, noncommital sons she talks a great deal about the lost civilizations of South America, the early days in Alaska, real estate in New York until they will agree with her and with each other later that she certainly is not out of her mind now.

Before her eldest daughter she sometimes cries for need of morphine and for the shame of it. No one wants to deprive her, but she would like to deprive herself. She, who has never been able to diet, budget, or curb her tongue, has always set her will against the impossible. She walked for thirty-five years after she was told she could not. She spent money all through the ruin of the depression until she had it again. She would not accept the reported losses during the war, and her children all came home. But even her will does not seem strong enough to defy addiction. The drug is not really at issue. She is addicted to life.

She speaks now with growing reverence about her husband who never saw the inside of a hospital. One day, while she waited for him in the car, he went into the bank and died. His best gestures had always been spontaneous. "Gifted" she calls him, with less irony than when he was alive.

And a little out of his mind from the beginning, surely, or he wouldn't have married her. (Don't imagine that's any one of us speaking. We have never been allowed to be on his side, and now there aren't any sides to take, really. Perhaps there never were.) St. Paul and his mother and some reckless gallantry of his own . . . well, she couldn't have been really beautiful, already twenty-six, six feet tall, with a man's stride which she had learned in the Yukon, in Salt Lake City, from the troops her father commanded. She did have curly auburn hair, high coloring, and ambition. So had he. They were second cousins. And she had been sent home to Kentucky to his own mother to be found a suitable husband. The indignity of it used to sharpen the edge of the courtship recounted. He had to be humiliated, too, a youngest son, spoiled, impractical, and, of course, sick with love. But, if she could not allow that he had rescued her from spinsterhood, neither could she force him so low as to be unworthy of her. He was gifted. That much, with his help, she proved to the world. He died in a bank, rich.

Yet now sometimes she says, "I should have learned to play the piano or to sing. It would have given him such pleasure," she who can't stand the sound of music. It makes her nervous. It always has.

The older twin has married a woman who does sing and play the piano. Obviously he is happier than our father was, but not as successful. And the second generation of that family, genetically so threatened, sing much too much of the time, not only in church and at home but in bars and on stages. It makes her nervous. It always has.

And this woman has nerves like an international communications system. Any impulse travels not simply along the inroads of her own body to arrive at gesture or malfunction but along transcontinental highways, over seas, even down dirt roads to find a home in one or more of us. We bite her nails, have her diarrhea, and her fainting spells. How can we then resent her indignation? Any sympathy from her would be self-pity, particularly for the other women of the family.

She is not as strict about females as the Dame of Sark, for instance, who tolerates no bitch but her own on the island. She could not be, having herself produced twice as many females as males. But her preferences, like her nervousness, are better expressed in us than in her. In the second and third generations the ratio of male to female is more than reversed. For this minority she has created special distinctions in language that go far beyond the conventions of English. The women, for instance, have migraine headaches while the men have bilious attacks, the first to be scorned as unreal weakness, the second to be tended with maternal concern. Girls are fussy, boys meticulous; girls are stubborn, boys tenacious; girls are uppity, boys proud; girls are smart, boys intelligent. And it's not just nouns and adjectives but verbs as well. Girls whine, boys protest; girls chatter, boys discuss; girls lie, boys invent. That is, when girls are allowed an active voice, when they are not trapped in the passive: seen not seeing, told not telling, chosen, not choosing, made, not making. But language is not unquestionably magic, and her specialized vocabulary for the women among us has not saved us from either her selfscorn or her power. Nor has it restored supremacy to the men among us. She has raised extraordinarily good husbands, faithful, fatherly, friendless.

NO? Is that a protest vote from the majority opposition? Or is it several individual counterclaims against the editorial we? We are trying to let all flowers bloom, but, of course, prose is not a flower bed, a space, but time, one thin line of it, an Indian file of syllables which can explore the field only moment by moment. Or fence it? The we is the fence, defining our limits. Some of us are climbing it, trying to get out. But point of view is a concentration camp of time, not space, and nobody can go until we are released. Not even she can go, as she has tried to, out of our time, not until we are released. And rebirth is never premature birth, not in this family. Get off that fence, John!

He isn't faithful. *He* isn't fatherly. And he has *lots* of friends, right over there on the other side who could turn we into they in a moment if he could just get there. John's been trying ever since he was a little boy, which wasn't for long, for even at three, when we left him at nursery school, he was mistaken for a first grader with a speech impediment because he couldn't pronounce his own full name properly, having at the end of it, as it did, III. The law could have changed his name but not the fact of being the third; he's by now himself admitted it with a son whose name ends IV. And, if that's sadistic, reality is. John's tried just about everything really. He used to say that Mrs. McGillicutty who lived in the garden arbor, which was really a bathroom where she was always taking a bath when we wanted to meet her, was his mother, and Mavon Dunner, three inches tall and asleep in a humming birds nest, his twin. Or John wasn't John at all but two bears, never one, always two of something. In the person of these two he could not be nice to little girls, shouted "grunty!" in the nursery school car pool and did it, not behind anyone's chair but on someone's front lawn, an act of real bravery because he was terrified of dogs. Oh, he could tell stories, but he wanted to tell them all backwards, and long after most of us had forgotten how to write, he was still busy writing poems to be read both forwards and backwards. And he wanted to plant a garden, a marvelous garden, from thousands of seeds tossed in a gunny sack, emptied slowly as he carried it, leaving a snail trail of carrot, fir tree, pumpkin, monkey pine, snap dragon, beet, bean, rhubarb and redwood tree, all by slow accident. Finally he wanted to construct a mobile, a huge mobile, to ride on. Perhaps he still does. But John has found out that he is our name carrier. He can call himself Typhoid Mary if he wants to. He can say that a name carrier is a name dropper in this family. He can even be right. He often is. But he can't get out.

She wasn't always as indulgent of John as she is now. "Your father could have been like John. He had it in him, but he also had me and God." In reverse order, historically anyway. According to family legend, our grandmother was a saint, a perhaps forgivable exaggeration to balance the other legend of a diabolical grandfather, who so acknowledged the sins of the world that he lost sight of God and was relieved of his church and his calling. Three of his sons gave their lives for his redemption. The fourth, our father, chose Mother and Mammon. Our grandmother, the saint, must have arranged it that way. Someone had to support the family.

Should something be said here about our dead father? He seems as out of place in these pages as he did in life, though none of us would deny the vital importance of his five seminal interruptions of our mother's life. (Could they have done it for fun? It's possible.) He traveled. He bought grapefruit groves and apartment houses. He liked women. The one rumored Lesbian in the family — Arachne isn't really her name, but our lawyer says leave it at that — claims her tastes come from him because he's the only one in the family who did like women as much as she does. But nobody, not even Arachne, wants to admit that he slept with any of them. He did fear God and Mother, and he was so blatant about it that he couldn't have been guilty, bills for women's hats, night clothes, and underwear always sent to the house for Mother to pay, snapshots of secretaries in bathing suits always falling out of family albums. And he wrote such unthreatening, romantic love letters, at one time or another, to all the women in the family, even some of the in-laws, that the source of his pleasure was obviously sentimental and esthetic. He liked giving women away, in church, to other men. It was, perhaps, his only fatherly instinct. But that is not to say that he was not proud of his family. He liked us enormously in photographs, particularly group photographs on important occasions, the twins' birthday, the christening of a child or a ship, the wedding of the youngest of us, the funeral of his mother, a victory at the Olympics. We hung on his office walls long before we were hung about her in her single, old age. He was also a giver of gifts. He once sent a letter to each member of the family: "If you had one wish in the world. . . ." But the replies must have disappointed him because it was our mother who then compiled a Christmas list which included writing paper with the family crest, roller skates, pipes, home permanents. That year he sent only one gift himself, a check to Arachne who had not answered his letter. She bought a cross for the altar of a church she didn't belong to, being a giver of gifts herself particularly to people she is suspicious of, like the Virgin Mary. Perhaps he knew that's what she'd do because he was always more generous to his brothers than to his children, installing a toilet in their house, a milking machine in the barn, a church on the back quarter. For lack of water, they flushed the toilet only once a week, a Sunday ceremonial after each one had used it. The milking machine was even less practical because the cows at the Kentucky farm were all neurotically hard milkers who responded to no one but the gentle, eldest brother singing Presbyterian hymns. The church was a Godsend, of course, and the brothers were ingenious at collecting and keeping a congregation. Once they spent a very wet day in the Ohio River reclaiming about a dozen who had been convinced by a traveling Baptist that total immersion was the only way to salvation. Our father was proud of his brothers' broadmindedness.

Our mother had another word for it. But, if she never suffered her brothers-in-law in silence, she tolerated their long visits with some devotion, teaching us, too, to be careful, contemptuous and kind. Mark, the second brother, the one who never married, lived with us for some time. All buck teeth and feet, he had a sluggish violence about him. He had a job for a while, reading meters on the Bowery, but every derelict he brought home to be saved made off with silver, an upstairs maid, or a piece of farm machinery, and finally, just when even our father was persuaded that Mark's job was an extravagance the family couldn't afford, he was fired for preaching temperance to his customers. He took singing lessons for a while, but Connecticut made him short of breath, he said. He went home to Kentucky.

So did we, singly and in groups, all generations of us until the last. Sometimes it was a disciplinary measure, sometimes a restorative, sometimes a treat. It was a place for children, perhaps because there weren't any there for a very long time until Luke, the third brother and the only ordained minister, in a sudden, unfastidious moment, impregnated his aging wife, who bore him a daughter as beautiful as any traveling salesman has ever described. She grew up between our first and second generations, a dirty joke, a crime, a myth, a secret, our only cousin, for whom our mother cannot feel sorry, with whom our father was obviously in love. She looks more like him than any of us do.

Which is to say that our father was beautiful? He had been, a fact somewhat embarrassing to those of us who have more traces of his vanity than his good looks. A beautiful father is, anyway, something of a bewilderment in this culture. Because of his beauty, we have to suspect our mother, for it is her weakness, not his. As a young woman, she must have looked not into the mirror but into his face for reassurance. Later, when we knew him, he moved about the house with averted eyes; yes, that's the phrase because it does call up archaic modesty along with guilt. He was a shy man, for all his enthusiasms, and he must sometimes have been filled with awe at his own audacity for having mounted the virgin goddess and ridden her into such matronly domesticity. Put it another way: his mother had hoisted him onto the biggest rocking horse of them all, and he couldn't get off; he didn't know how. But why belittle him? He did stand taller than she; he was more beautiful. He was gifted as mortal men are gifted. He is our trace of humanity, which is the attractiveness we have, and we all have it, even those of us who take the mole hill of our Olympus most seriously. While some make whispered claims to be children of the gods, we are relieved to have proof of a mortal father, John I, the beloved, farm boy tycoon, obsessed with grapefruit groves and toilets (apartment buildings are the palaces of democracy, housing the thrones of private men), women and churches. Did we say he was bald? He was. He had even more androgen than our mother.

Yet with all that hormonal magnificence, between them they produced twice as many females as males, until the second and third generations. The reversal of ratio has not corrected the original error, for the two sons of the first generation produced only one son apiece in the second, and of those two only John III has a son. He won't have any more, not legitimate ones anyway. And his cousin is our literary critic whose celibacy is a greater disgrace than John III's promiscuity. Simply, our women bear sons, our men conceive daughters; therefore, out of six in the first generation, only two carry our father's name; out of eighteen in the second generation, still only two carry our father's name; and in the third generation, which stands at twenty-six, only one carries our father's name, John IV. Our father is dead. His name is dying.

Six plus eighteen plus twenty-six equals fifty. It takes something approaching black magic to reduce a name to one hope out of fifty. Our mother will not be shamed by this fact, "You are all mine," she says, for it isn't her name that is dying. It committed suicide on the day she was married, and she survived it. She still survives it, in herself and in us. She is no one's property; she is the country of our birth.

All stand to pledge allegiance to the united states of our mother, numen of a continent, whom we cannot escape from sea to shining sea or even overseas to lands she will not let us live in, to wars she will not let us die in. We are not nameless. We are America, from the mountains to the valleys to the oceans white (mark white) with foam, god bless our mother, land, our HOME SWEET HOME where we see through the night that our bombs are still there.

All bow heads in prayer: our mother, who art on earth, hallowed be any name in this kingdom of thy will.

All clap hands.

All fall down.

No one stands alone.

That's the trouble. For together we are bound to con-fuse religious and political rituals, and all our voices make it difficult to determine whether we are in church or officers' club, in town meeting or sanitorium, in crib or king-sized bed. Any general statement of our issue is obviously so much counterfeit currency, but it's all we have to spend. No one stands alone, not in this cold war corps of begotten fidelity. We are born to carry on.

And in precisely that confusion of military and sexual terminology we do, from generation to generation. Orestes and Arachne, who are also twins, have theories about both themselves and the original twins, their father (the younger) and their uncle (John II), whom we all call the Captain and the Colonel, retiring ranks for retiring men. Male twins are supposed to be culture heros, claiming one mortal and one immortal parent, whose gifts include unusual intelligence, second sight, success in love and in war.

"But they lose their power," Orestes reads carefully, "if they eat food prepared by a menstruating woman."

Our mother either observed the taboo or triumphed over it to provide America with one ruler over the land and one ruler over the sea. She offered her twin sons to West Point and Annapolis before they were full grown, a tradition that has been observed in all generations of the family to avoid the danger of disqualification. She offered her four daughters, as we have all offered ours in turn, to her sons' classmates so that America might also have goddesses of earth and water. By these devices she also created a friendly rivalry between the services, a sport that has, from time to time, rocked both the family and the nation. The struggles between culture heros always have.

Colonel John II, though a handsome and unhairy man, has always been in danger of selling his birthright to the younger twin, and some of us think it not at all unlikely that

73

one day he will have his head knocked into the lap of our dead father by the youngest and most energetic of us. He has Esau's appetites for pottage and firearms. He did win the war single-handed, having lost the other one and all his men on a strategically insignificant little island in the Pacific, a costly victory only because the Navy shelled instead of covering its own invading forces. The Colonel was given a medical discharge, the Captain a desk job in Washington for a decent period before he was retired.

"If a woman brings forth twins a second time," Orestes reads carefully, "the country will be destroyed."

It is not hard to imagine, but Orestes and Arachne, cognizant of those dangers, limit their own mysterious powers to an influence for evil over other members of the family and to a gift for curing wounds and injuries. As children at the Kentucky farm, they practiced their craft of curing colic by kicking sick animals seven times in the stomach, an experiment which did not win them the blessing of our father's brothers, who, under the influence of a Presbyterian god, did not extend brutality to animals.

"Being a female twin," Arachne discovers, "I will never be successful at cooking tamales or squash."

She has, as a result, never cooked at all. But she has other gifts, our giver of gifts, our maker of the web, frail, perfect net to catch a nourishment of enemies, who, bound in silk, become the episodes which teach the errors of the gods.

"One twin is often born inhuman, a snake or a crab," or a spider?

"Twins are often sacrificed," miscarried?

"The persecution of twins and their mother leads to their being avengers of mother, sister, betrothed, or wife," or, in a matriarchal subculture, avengers of a father?

74

Not the Captain and the Colonel, certainly. They are our mother's beloved sons, who have struggled in her womb for the privilege of being the first born, who have struggled in the world to be the first blessed by her. It is into her lap each would like his head finally to fall. And we can accept their struggling in womb and world, but we speculate with moral horror at what must have gone on between Orestes and Arachne. And so must they, who did not, after all, choose to be so intimately enclosed for nine months, prenatal swimmers in the same sea. They have really neither challenged nor avenged anybody, but they behave as if they had, and rumors of their impotence, guilt and defiance threaten the whole family with catastrophe. To be related to a male literary critic and a female artist is almost as embarrassing as to have had a beautiful father.

The threat of twins, both the two sets mentioned and the mythical miscarriage of foetal sacrifice, continues. The women of the family are very careful not to eat double almonds, double yolked eggs, or any of the other ritual foods, but there are already two new sets of twins in the third generation. Publically, of course, we are proud of them, for our mother is proud of them, liking almost everything in quantity. She makes of their forced intimacy a virtue she would have us all practice. With uncertainty, nervousness, and circumspection, we do.

Even John III, who would like to debase or deny our spiritual incest, has been unable to do so, for, while he refuses to love his relatives, his wives do. His first wife became so enamoured of the family that she divorced him at the moment of his most confident rebellion. When he married again, a woman over six feet tall like all his female relatives, he decided to keep the marriage a secret. It was impossible to hide the woman herself, except at a family gathering where she would be inconspicuous; therefore he allowed her to share an apartment with Arachne so that she might attend various reunions as Arachne's friend. She grew so fond of Arachne, however, that his own relationship with her was threatened. We thought his jealousy so distasteful, particularly when he made scenes in front of his first wife who also attended family reunions as mother of John IV, that he had no choice finally but to confess to his second marriage, at which moment his second wife confessed that she was about to divorce him. She continues to move among us inconspicuously as Arachne's friend. John III, our name carrier, attends alone or not at all. He imagines that our incestuous source, parents who were second cousins, explains our mass idiocy and deformity.

There is not an idiot among us. Very few of the women have been given university educations, but they have all been educated by the educated men they married. Not one is unable to balance a check book, drive a car, take advantage of foreign servants, tyrannize over the wives of junior officers and manipulate the wives of senior officers. They all have Irish linen, silver tea services, and oriental carpets. And most of them can say "How much?" and "No" in at least five languages. Their ignorance of politics is not so much a limitation as a fidelity to the traditions of the old Army and real Navy. Their indifference to the arts and social welfare is a mark of discipline rather than laziness. They are the good earth of self-reliant conservatism, breeding bright sons for each new war.

Our men are intelligent. Not one has been killed in action or deprived of a pension. Some of our in-laws have even made money. We are all looked up to.

Height is not a deformity. To be born at least twenty-three inches long and to achieve at least six feet is our proud expectation. Not one of us has failed. And we are secure enough in our superiority to admit the little self-consciousnesses of adolescence. The boys are inclined toward clownishness, chinning themselves on rafters and street signs. The girls are a little aggressive, offering to hold doors and carry luggage for small, male strangers. Each of us during this period has probably suffered a momentary disloyalty to our inheritance, but once we are acclimated, discovering that the air is not really thinner nor the weather more turbulent, we enjoy our advantage. We take advantage easily, particularly when we are together. By ourselves, we take exception, being exceptional.

It is a privilege to be excluded not from the rank but from the file of men who are foreigners, yankees, niggers, and midgets. But we are neither blind nor unkind. We can see the little people. Each has his little charity, as our mother has her coat hangers. We support such selective institutions as the Home for White, Southern, Unwed, Presbyterian Mothers and the Home for White, Southern, Disabled Officers of West Point and Annapolis. We also contribute to any disaster fund for Florida Fruit Growers and New York Real Estate Owners. We do not contribute to organizations for America First or Moral Rearmament just as we don't put our money in broad investment funds. We make a clear distinction between opinion and fact, knowing that, except for the military, the world is usually run by amateurs. We believe in control, in our own authority, because we have a history of victories.

ALL'S WELL IN WINNEMUCCA, Mother. She likes to know that even now. Whenever any one of us passes through, we stop to send the message: ALL'S WELL IN WINNE-MUCCA, Mother. If there has just been a hold-up or a murder, the telegraph clerk may take a skeptical view of our reporting, but she does not understand that our mother wants to be assured of just one thing: that her father did put down the last Indian uprising there. We look for federal troops and redskins. The bare plains and hills are still. Colonel John II, on his way from Washington, D.C., to the south Pacific early in 1942, was almost arrested in Winnemucca, and the message went through censored: ALL'S WELL IN XXXXXXXXXXX, Mother, but she understood. "Each war ends war," she said. When Arachne cabled, early in 1947, ALL'S WELL IN HIROSHIMA, Mother, she nodded with the same vision. Redskins, yellow skins, black skins: each war ends war and extends the dynasty.

The dust, radioactive and otherwise, settles again, but we do not. Does it really matter that we can't go home again? Any of us? Our tradition is transience, in war or peace. Family seats on this continent turn into old people's homes, private schools, power generators and super highways even before our mothers have hysterectomies, our fathers heart attacks, ourselves commissions or children. We move in and out of houses even more rapidly than presidents and first ladies move in and out of the White House. Army posts and naval bases provide the same kind of continuity: one wide, prisoner-tended lawn, one set of uncertain back stairs, one basement toilet is much like another. We learn to be at home without having a home to go to, except our mother. She has wanted it so, offering a security no wider than her own great width, wider than the world. She has taught us to occupy seats on planes, park benches, and chairlifts with the confidence of permanent reservation. There isn't a seat to set a bottom on that isn't as uncomfortable and reassuring as the family pew, which our father set up in Kentucky and our mother sold out from under us the day after we laid him to rest in the one piece of ground that should have been incontestably his. She also sold the Connecticut shingle chateau, but that had already been loaned out as a home for retarded children in the thirties, a club for officers in the forties, our mother's pity and patriotism more eloquent than the motivating financial reversals. (Our father was slow to get into war industry.) We never went home to Connecticut to our own simple memories, the ghostly games of Mongolian idiots threading through our dances and riots, mindless nightmares among our own sweet dreams; and later, in the service, we returned to beds made unheroic by unknown soldiers who had probably, without the proper sense of profession, died. The Kentucky farm had given us a certain softness of speech, rural sexuality, and southern pride which the real landscape only threatened. It was not an estate but a small country slum, bottom land of the Ohio, silt and sewage of river myths we remember better for not having to die there. Perhaps even our father rests in greater peace for having been sold down that river. No one wants to go home again. We pass through, reporting: ALL'S WELL, Mother. ALL'S WELL.

She used to take the tour of inspection herself, stepping from child to child across the continent. Those of us not directly in her path always gathered along the route for whistle stop love and campaign promises. She liked the train, an inverted Mrs. Roosevelt who never failed to make the porters homesick for the north and west they traveled through, herself at home anywhere because of her children or her own childhood, there in Salt Lake City, for instance, where as a girl she had gone through the unconsecrated Temple. This is the place. Every place is the place. We all heard ALL'S WELL IN WINNEMUCCA one winter when she passed through. She did not mention the blizzard which not even she could put down. John III left the crap table at

Harold's Club to meet the train in Sparks. "Get off, Mother." But she would not. What Donner had dared she could not fail to do. "It's rumored that they finally ate each other, Mother," but what began as a warning sounded instead like a promise: you old cannibal. The train reached the summit but did not cross it.

"Where do you think you're going?" the troopers asked him at Truckee.

"To dinner with Mother."

On snow shoes with a dog sled, he went in with the rescue crews to find her. She was pleased to see him, who had left not so much as one toe in the snow all that long way up, but she turned down the dog sled, being too heavy and immobile a cargo. He had dinner with her, sandwiches and hot coffee, was interviewed by the press, helped to subdue a drug addict in violent withdrawal, and then discussed chances of survival with the engineers. He would have stayed on the train, but the dogs had to be returned.

"They say the train will get to California, Mother."

"I believe it."

He walked back down the mountain, leaving Paul Bunyan tracks in the snow, and read over morning coffee, under a very flattering picture of himself, the story of the one irresponsible tourist who had arrived on the scene with an empty dog sled, demanding a share of the food brought in for the survivors. Then he took a telephone call from his uncle, the Captain, in Berkeley.

"I see you had dinner with Mother last night."

"Since I was in the neighborhood, it was the least I could do."

"Is she well?"

"Yes, she seems to be fine, but she may be a little late into Berkeley."

"We understand."

"Well, all the best, Captain."

"All the best to you, John."

It was tough competition, but the Captain took up the challenge two nights later when the train finally did arrive in Berkeley, where the storm had slopped that bowl of bay over the shoreside tracks and was firing rain from a tilted, almost perpendicular sky. There was no shelter. There were no wheel chairs. The Captain drove his car right onto the station platform, relieved two exhausted porters of the bulk of our mother and carried her off. She was not ungrateful, but she is used to that kind of attention. What she wanted to recall of that journey was John III, elegant on snow shoes, at Donner Summit in a blizzard, dropping in for dinner and offering her a ride on a dog sled.

"Like the old days in Alaska."

"You certainly have an amazing, marvelous family," her friends all exclaim.

"I didn't reckon on raising any fools."

It is her own reckoning that matters. When she went on to Texas to look into the broken engagement of an uncertain granddaughter, she did not have to listen to any explanations.

"He wasn't your sort of man anyway."

"Grandfather wasn't your sort either," the girl answered in perverse grief.

"Ah, but marrying him made all the difference."

Home is where the heart is, darlin', not necessarily deep in the heart of Texas. Simply choose to brood over any state from marriage to Maine, and that makes all the difference.

We brood, doves and madmen, old hens and soldiers, over the amazing landscape of her authority, without choice. For her 'to be committed' is a pledge, for us a confinement. Her 'conviction' is a belief she holds, ours a judgment we would like to avoid; therefore we restlessly populate the green, unquiet neighborhoods of the vast middle class (whether military or civilian) carefully isolated between the madhouse and the jail. But while others are advised by refugee psychiatrists (whose uncertain command of English is the triumphant cliche) to practice moderation in all things, are warned by politicians against the passions of the lunatic fringe, are prompted by ministers to tolerance and understanding which grow out of group anxiety and group guilt, we will be neither committed to nor convicted of any ideal but our mother. She does not sympathize with either those isolated from the law or those isolated in it. She is the law, which cannot identify with poets in asylums, rapists in jail, any young man in the grave, which cannot feel pity and terror because it does not admit that, in a democracy, anyone who comes within the law can lose his mind, his trial or his life; therefore we are not her victims but her heroes.

Here's a bit of subversive sympathy, siblings: there have been presidents who have lived through their terms of office. There are Negro leaders who have died of old age, still black. There are ministers who have preached in unbombed churches and gone to heaven in their own sweet time. Pound's second asylum was the whole of Italy. Chessman was killed, but the Birdman of Alcatraz died of his own accord, and prisons all over the country are setting up typewriters in death row so that men can earn their own defense with badly written best sellers. (But reprieve is only temporary relief from the law.) Well, avoid signing contracts, joining organizations, contesting anyone's will, dead or alive, and obey our mother, who has done all these things for us and is not afraid. There is, even without choice, one kind of independence: if we must obey out of both habit and necessity, we can also co-operate willfully, unnecessarily. That is called love.

82

Which damned well will lead us into the madhouse or the jail, finally into the grave! Unless we become her comic rather than her tragic heroes, self-nominated, self-elected, against all tradition to our public schools, committed in a mother we are willing not to die but to live for in ridiculous, culpable power and delight. Comic heroes who live for their mothers ought to set an entirely new fashion, no Oedipal eye for such appetites, nor sick, silver cords, but picaresque morality of gigantic proportions. And if there has to be a little suffering here and there, let it be erotic sadism. The Colonel's hand, for instance, was never anything but a comic device, and, if he finally loses his head as well, he'll still be larger than life. We all will, even the women, who, though they have lately taken birth control pills even more regularly than tranquilizers, are still some sort of symbol of life. We are obviously a traveling comedy, a road show, a side show, that's the whole show, because this is the place. Every place is the place of the unconsecrated temple, into which our priestess mother has taken us, not to pray but to play out our huge, silly, heroic lives in the shadow of all unblessedness. ALL'S WELL IN WINNEMUCCA, Mother, is the tune we have to dance to, the fact we take our stance to, for it is American historical garbage out of which our nursery rhymes and myths must finally come.

Are we ready? One two three, up to and including fifty strong, if we can keep Orestes from taking up residence outside the country so that his citizenship prevents him from being a citizen, if we can keep John III from having anything but babies by that colored maid of his, if we can keep Arachne from enlisting two other fates to spin, wrap, and cut us down to a fly-sized tragedy, we may really learn all the routines of joy.

The trouble is that depression was the natural climate

not only of *the* thirties but of *our* thirties, through which the first generation passed in the forties not without lasting consequences, through which the second generation thinks it may never get, sharing premature careers, mortgages, transfers, and Mother. We are all busy, in every generation, foreclosing each other's earlier illusions, which may be a comic routine but takes its toll of even the funniest heroes. The joy ride, the travel grant, the Pacific theatre, become tours of duty with armies of occupation and early retirement for one generation, become the commuter trains of civilian resignation for the next. So shall we say that the war joy has been a kill joy, leaving us all unaccountably alive with more rank than peace has use for, more power than lawn mower, golf club, personal enemy or wife can accommodate? Frame and hang our medals on the wall, like our faces, small suns for small sons to reflect on. If there's not much chance of killing a Russian, if Cuba and Red China are to be intimidated with unmilitary starvation, there are still hopes of a larger peace army, who can set up and overthrow the same government during a lull in sponsored civil war. But where do old soldiers go to die? Is there an elephant graveyard for us, too?

Oh, Elephant Mother, who has taught us not to pray for peace in our time, do you know where you are going, where you will lead us? Is there under the tree or under the carpet itself or up in the sky, beyond your blimp shadow, some place to stop? Must we always, following, pass through in the shadow your murderous life casts on some one else's grave home? Is all really well?

We do believe in our own authority, don't we? We, who have been coupling and competing from the womb, to spring ungrown into a world born by women where men fuck and fight for holy honors, clean language at the dinner table, and a respected old age? We, who are living through that world, expecting to outgrow it into some giant peace of, of course our own authority, which is. . . ?

Our mother. How can we allow her to die, source and measure, our landscape and salvation? Yet there is a rumor that she is dying, not spectacularly now so that we can rally to rally her, but slowly, almost privately. Listen, this woman has been dying for the last fifty-seven years, a dying that began on the day she married our father. It has been so gradual a decline that it might be thought of — and usually is — as her living. But the big, blimp goddess will not live forever. Her heart is a tired sack in the tired sack of her body. Intravenous television cannot feed her mind much longer, nor can the urine bottle contain forever the waste of years. Her tree of life, her grand delusion, is really this forest of family, these tall, shallow-rooted trees, trying to live in a cold place, the place of her dying, threatened ourselves by the rumor of that last high wind. We must go to her one by one, quickly, for judgment, for blessing, for love. March on the beloved. She is mortal.

A Walk
by Himself

"What in hell do you think you're doing?" William Miller demanded. "What in hell do you think I'm doing, working my ass off so that you can crap on your exams because you're too busy screwing your girl to study? So that you can get money off me to pay your court fines for cracking up somebody's car? Is that what you think? Is it?"

Bill sat forward on the couch, looking away from his father. He lit a china table lighter, stared at the flame, then blew at it.

"Stop that! Look at me."

Bill turned his head slowly and looked up at his father, a big, crude, powerful man in his early fifties.

"You're to say what the hell you think you're doing."

"I don't know," Bill answered and reached for the lighter again.

"What do you mean, you don't know? It don't take no university education. Any damn fool can see what you're doing. You're wasting every goddamned opportunity in the world. What do you think I moved west for? I had a damned good farm, and I like farming, but, when a man's a farmer, that's all his kids can be. I wanted my kids to be anything they wanted; so I found country where they could. Look at this country!" William Miller gestured at the wall. "By God, you can be any damn thing you want here if you got education. So I'm educating my kids. So I'm giving you four damn years to be an engineer, four years when you ought to be working to pay back all I already done for you. And what are you? What are you?"

"I don't know."

"You don't know? Then I'll tell you. You're a fool. You haven't got no guts. You haven't got no imagination. I show you trees could make a man rich. I show you where you build a road and own half the goddamned province. I show you an ocean full of fish, just waiting to be caught. Look at this world! Look at it! There's more work and more money than there is men to get it. And you can't think of nothing to do but crap on exams and crack up cars and screw girls. I don't know why in hell a world wastes itself on you."

"Neither do I."

"I'll damn well take you out of the university, show you what it's like not to have no education, no car, show you what it's like to work for a living."

"All right."

"Then we'll see what a big goddamned man your girl thinks you are. Don't think I won't, neither. What have you got to say for yourself?"

"Nothing."

"Nothing? You damn well got to say you'll do better."

"I'll try."

"You'll do more than try, I'll tell you that. You don't go out no more, only Saturday nights. You study your books every damned night. You don't drive your car, only to school and back, only Saturday nights for Peggy. And you stop treating her like a tramp."

"I don't treat her like a tramp."

"Don't crap me. I know what you do. You lay her when you feel like it and don't give her no time when you don't. You'll get no sympathy from me when you knock her up. You'll marry her and go to work."

"I intend to marry her."

"Oh, you do? On what? On her salary? Let a woman work for you?"

"When I get out. When I get a job."

"At the rate you're getting out, you'll be working in no time."

"Maybe so."

"Maybe so. I don't know. Nothing. I tell you this, boy, the big blowout's over. Right now you're starting at those books. Right now you're definitely knowing something."

"I promised Peggy I'd go over there."

"Well, go unpromise her."

Bill got up and walked around the couch toward the phone in the front hall.

"Well," William Miller said, "take the books over there." He threw a half smoked cigarette into the fireplace, walked heavily out of the room into the kitchen. He did not speak to his wife. He slammed out the back door, and then, in the drive, a car engine turned over.

Bill went into the kitchen. "I guess I'll take off."

"I fixed you and Peggy a picnic lunch," his mother said quietly. "It's such a nice day."

"Thanks, Mom." He stood for a moment, looking at the back of her head. Then he picked up the large paper bag on the drain board. "Well, I'll see you."

"Bill?"

"Yeh?" he said, turning back toward her.

"Be careful, won't you?"

"Yeh, I'll be careful."

"I don't ever want you to be sorry, Bill, when it's too late."

"Yeh, Mom, okay."

Names that were curses from his father, warnings that were threats from his mother: he carried these out of the house around the vacuum at the center of him, heavy with a pressure, a foreboding gravity he did not quite believe in. He had cracked up his car, flunked three of his five exams and not seen Peggy for over a week. All these had once been terrors to him which he had not quite believed in. Yet now that they had happened, he could not see why he had been afraid. His father had paid the court fine and the bill for the repairs on the car. The university had not thrown him out, nor had his father refused to pay tuition for the spring term. Bill did feel guilty about not having seen Peggy, but she did not criticise him. She was afraid she might lose him. It was her fear that had made him angry and then indifferent. She had no pride. But even in his boredom, Bill could not cut himself off from Peggy. She was the last of the crumbling symbols which had last fall made up the whole structure of his purpose. If he turned from her, there would be really nothing left of the world he planned to live in that mattered at all. He did not know how to confront absolute emptiness.

Bill got into his car and turned on the ignition. At once the radio, never turned off, whined the last of a commercial at him. Impatient, he backed out of the drive without looking, jammed his brakes only as he heard the shriek of tires and violent horn of the slowly moving car he had almost hit. Its driver swore at him. Bill did not bother to answer. He swung roughly into his own lane and pressed the accelerator to the floor. Speed would sharpen his senses, extend his power, give the present some challenge and purpose. In it he could forget for a moment that he was in no hurry to meet Peggy.

"I don't ever want you to be sorry, Bill, when it's too late." Once he could have heard his mother, making sense. But now he had flunked, cracked up a car, ignored his girl, and he wasn't sorry. Perhaps his mother meant something bigger. He might marry the wrong girl or kill a man. Then, surely, he would be sorry, and it would be too late. But how could he know he would be sorry until it was too late? Bill Miller did not really believe in the grief his mother was afraid he would come to.

He swung hard around a corner. Something big and terrible had to happen to him. But what would be the purpose? He imagined Peggy telling him that she was pregnant. Then he would have to marry her, get a job, but the martyrdom was unreal. He might, after all, not marry her. Perhaps he would kill a man. But it was such a ridiculous idea. Well, just say he had killed a man. He would have to go to prison. There, cut off from the world, he would write a book about kids like himself to show them. But show them what? What would he know from killing a man that he did not know now?

Driving through the city, indifferent to his direction, Bill felt his mind a maze of streets, down which his thought turned reckless, frantic, deadended, until he knew there was no way out, no direction that mattered. Indifference settled, then flared into frustration, into speed, and he dared the road to present an obstacle worth his grief.

A small, black dog trotted away from a child into the path of Bill's car. He would not brake, instead called all his skill with his foot hard on the gas to avoid hitting it. The thud, then the cry of the child, announced his failure. Bill jammed on the brakes, swearing, and was about to get out of the car when he saw the child's mother brought out of the house by the cry. Bill had been speeding. He would be blamed, perhaps taken to court again. He yanked the gear into first, dug out, wheeled around the corner and drove fifty miles an hour through the quiet residential streets of the city, a marvelous excitement in him. Not to be caught, not to be blamed was so clear a purpose that he laughed. Nothing would happen unless he allowed it to happen. He could refuse, escape anything.

The grand criminal. He'd killed a kid's dog. He was driving slowly now past the rows of box houses toward the shore road. He turned and pulled off the road where a path went down the cliff to the bay, and then he got out. He stood looking out over the water first toward the north shore and then toward the sea, the vast empty limit of the world. The beach below him was bright with fine, shallow snow and still. It was too cold now for many people to be out, but Bill decided he'd go get Peggy and bring her here for the picnic. They could wrap up in the blankets he carried in the trunk. They could feed the gulls. It was only a dog, after all.

He got back in the car and drove toward Peggy's house, wondering if he should tell her about killing the dog. No, of course he wouldn't. Peggy would just cry and then tell him it wasn't his fault, try to make him feel better. Why couldn't she ever know that sometimes he didn't want to feel better, wished he could feel worse?

Bill dawdled to keep her waiting, took the long way, let an old lady and a dozen school kids cross a street, bought some gas. As he waited at the filling station, Bill watched a man leading a blind boy across the road. As they walked, the man talked to the boy, describing the corner, the gas station, the cars on the road, the people they passed. The boy, his white cane tentative in his hand, nodded vigorously all the while.

"Look at this world! Look at it! I don't know why the hell a world wastes itself on you." Bill had always thought he saw the world his father saw until a few months ago when gradually, without knowing why, he began to realize that he did not believe in his father's vision. The great forests did not really seem a challenge to him. And the sea, a great wonder and potential to his father, was for Bill the edge of the world, a dead end. What would happen to that blind kid if he began to doubt the world his father told him about? What would happen when he decided one day to go for a walk by himself?

The garage attendant asked to check the oil and water.

"Sure."

It was another delay, but Peggy wouldn't say anything about his being late. She'd smile at him as if she were almost surprised to see him, as if he were early.

"And you stop treating her like a tramp."

Well, if she minded the way he treated her, she could just say so. He'd walk out. But would he really? Where would he go? What other girl would be like Peggy? He certainly didn't want a girl nagging him. He certainly didn't want a girl who had a great big thing about virginity. He certainly didn't want a girl who thought she knew it all.

It was another blind alley. Bill pressed down on the accelerator. Anything was better than listening to himself.

"Well, here's the young genius," Peggy's father said as he opened the door. "I thought the law probably got you again."

Bill laughed. This was a man he really did hate, and knowing it, feeling it in him so strong, made him easy. Peggy needed him.

"Hi," she said as she came into the hall.

"Hi. We're going on a picnic. Get your coat."

"Picnic?" her father echoed, "on a day like this?"

"That's right," Bill said, not looking at him, watching Peggy, who was getting her coat from the hall closet. It was like her not to have to go upstairs, to be all ready to do whatever he wanted. She looked to him like a little kid, standing there reaching for her coat. She had on the soft pink sweater Bill liked, a grey skirt and sturdy shoes. She must have known he would want to be outdoors.

"Well, don't think you'll stay home from work with one of your colds," Peggy's father said to her back, and then to Bill, "Some people make a living, you know."

"Peggy won't have to much longer," Bill said, bold at the beginning of his sentence, his voice trailing off.

"Oh?" The look on her father's face was filthy.

"Come on, Peggy, let's go."

"I'm ready."

"Mind yourself," her father said. "You come damn close to not having a roof over your head last time."

Bill wanted to hit him, to knock him down, and keep hitting him until he could never look at them like that again. Why didn't he? He didn't because he didn't want Peggy cut off from her family. He didn't want to marry her. Bill walked by him, guiding Peggy out onto the front porch, cleared his throat and spat into the bushes. The door slammed behind him.

The sun was warm as they climbed down the cliff, but on the beach the wind was cold against them, the ground cold under them, and they walked a long way, Peggy carrying the lunch, Bill the blankets, before they found a place sheltered from the wind and sunny. Bill climbed about the rocks until he found what he wanted. Then he cleared the snow from a small shelf, put down the canvas, then a blanket, and helped Peggy up.

"I'm starved!" he said.

"I love Saturdays," she said, as she moved close to him and helped cover them with blankets.

"Let's have some of that lunch." He reached across her for the bag. "Dad blew his top this morning."

"What about?"

"Everything." Bill unwrapped the sandwiches, handed her one.

"Is anything going to happen?"

"Naw. Nothing ever happens." Bill took a bite of his sandwich and began to talk while he chewed. "He just blows up, yells around, and then forgets about it."

"I wish my dad did that."

"He been at you again?"

"No, not really."

"You're to tell me."

"It only makes you mad."

"You're damned right it makes me mad! What did he do?"

"Nothing, Bill, really. I only wish he was like your dad, that's all."

"Well, you're to tell me." Bill took another great bite of his sandwich.

"I will."

"Dad's making me stay in week nights until my grades are up."

"Oh."

"We can go out on Saturdays just the same." Bill reached into the bag. "Want an egg?"

"No thanks."

"You ought to eat an egg," Bill decided, handing her one.

"All right."

That was it. He wanted her to say just what she said, but it made him mad. She sounded scared of him. Maybe she was, or maybe she just had no mind of her own. She didn't care what she did. She was stupid.

"I shouldn't see so much of you anyway," Bill said. "Don't get anything done. Anyway, we might get bored."

This time she didn't answer. He looked down at her to see if he had hurt her, but her face was turned away from him. She was eating her egg, and all he could see was her small, cold hand.

"Aw, Peggy," he said, putting an arm around her. "You know I'm kidding. I never get bored with you." He cupped his hand under her and lifted her onto his lap. "There, that's warmer, isn't it?"

"Mmmm," she said, as she caught the sliding lunch bag and put it down where she had been sitting. Her shifting weight was lovely against him.

"Why don't you get your hands warm?"

It was great to have a girl like Peggy. She was really a nice girl, but she wasn't a prude. She liked it. She really did. And she let you know it.

"There are people coming along, Bill," she said, pulling away from him.

"Shit!" He got up and looked down at the beach. She was right. This was no place to horse around. But where was there a place in broad daylight? No wonder people finally just gave up and got married.

"Let's walk," he said irritably.

"Okay."

Let's stand on our heads. Let's eat sand. Let's walk out to sea. Okay, she'd say. Okay, Bill, let's. What was the use? Peggy wasn't his kind of girl. He needed somebody else, somebody who'd tell him just how stupid he was, just how lazy, just how rotten. He did treat her like a tramp. He did use her and then ignore her. He didn't want to marry her. His father was right. He hadn't any guts or imagination. He was a fool, and he needed somebody to tell him so who was important enough to make him mad.

They had walked to the edge of the water, where they stood looking out over the bay to the mountains on the north shore, to the beginnings of the forest.

"Trees could make a man rich," Bill said.

"Trees?"

"Yeh, trees." But what did he care about trees? They were nice to look at, but he didn't want to cut them down. He didn't want to build roads or bridges. Oh, he'd like money. It would be fine to have money, but you had to work so hard, care so much to get it. "Let's feed the gulls."

"They're greedy birds," Peggy said.

"Sure, so let's feed them. I like to see them really go after it."

He opened the lunch bag, handed Peggy a sandwich, took one himself. Then they walked along the edge of the water where there was no snow, where the salt softened the sand and crusted the shells and pebbles. Bill threw the bread out into the water and watched the gulls, grey and white like the sky and the snow, swoop heavily, clumsily down at the water, fighting for bits. Peggy dropped her bread along the shore so that they began to be followed by swarms of gulls, a great racket of wings in the cold wind. Bill walked faster to move away from Peggy, and, as was her habit, she sensed his need to move away and did not try to keep near him. He climbed out onto a ridge of rock that stretched far out beyond the water line into the bay. There he stood alone, tossing bits of bread, until the air around him was wild with gulls. Into their flapping awkward midst came a fleet of blackbirds, swift and small and dark against the grey sky and water. They were shy of the gulls, shy of the water, but frantic with a winter hunger. He watched them dare the gulls, watched the gulls attack. Fine, greedy birds, determined to have their own. Bill tore up the last sandwich to give them something to fight over. Then, as he watched, he reached into the bag and found the last hard boiled egg. His hand closed around it. A cloud of blackbirds dropped toward the water. The gulls cried out. Bill cocked his arm and hurled the egg. The cloud drew up into the air. The gulls scattered. There on the water with the last of the bread, one small blackbird rocked with the tide for a moment and then began to sink.

Bill stood shocked, then turned and looked back toward Peggy. She had her back to him. She had not seen. The relief he felt made him weak. Then he wanted to sit down on the rocks and cry, cry all the grief out, all the shame for the failure, for the crack up, for the dog he'd killed, for the bird, for Peggy. It was big and terrible, this need to cry in him, as if nothing would ever happen to him but crying.

He ran along the rocks, down on the beach, and back to Peggy.

"Listen, Peggy," he said. "Listen, let's get married."

"Okay," she said, her face so grateful he felt he could not keep from crying, "okay, Bill, let's."

The Furniture
of Home

It was too simple — that is, too defensive — to say everyone else had sold out. If someone had suggested to Paul that he was the one who hadn't bought in, he could have attacked. Without that challenge, his hostility would be ill mannered, nothing else. In a month at home, not even his father had asked a direct question. Why should he really? Paul had not cost him a penny for eight years. On fellowships and grants and odd jobs he had studied and traveled, getting a degree in architecture at his own pace, being somewhat damaged but not broken by the system. He managed that by being talented and slightly foreign. How talented he was, however, remained to be tested or not. How foreign he was he did not know until he got home.

A Canadian student in New York does not have to burn his draft card or march for civil rights which he himself does not enjoy. Yet he can live mistaken for the citizen he is not, his loyalist blood unrecognized. There is no pressure to marry. In fact, he has to leave the country to work. But a nearly trained Canadian can work in England, foreign relative without either burden or blessing of accent. And return to another grant, prize money, choose to live simply and alone. . . or not. Paul lived briefly with a friend, even more briefly with a woman, and finally alone with his thesis, over a store, next to a fire escape, until it was written. A defeat of a kind, his degree, 'the ticket', but he endured it with some detachment, achieved with rum or blended whiskey on hard evenings.

Now, at home, among all too recognizable friends, he could not apologize for what he had achieved. He had to use it instead as a bridge into their new living rooms. All the friends he called on had houses they did not like but were proud of, and most of them had wives who could be similarly described. Conversations were expedient or nostalgic. Paul, without a job and uncommitted to his profession, could be nostalgic but not in the same way his friends were, who had lost things gradually before their eyes.

In Paul's own neighborhood, he visited a house where his best friend had once lived among a litter of brothers and sisters in a dormered and divided attic or out in an overgrown garden of temporary paths and permanent mysteries. The present tenants, a teacher Paul had had and his wife, wanted him to admire the new master bedroom and bath that took up the whole top floor, the limestone walks and ordered rockeries. He did, paying some relieving penance against his outraged taste, but he could not resist showing them where George's room had been, how they might, if they peeled away their embossed wallpaper, find the black ceiling of his boyhood.

Experiences like this made Paul question himself as much as the people around him. What had he expected after eight years? Had he really thought that in his own country, in his own city, he would find people like himself, trained in detachment, valuing nothing but that, a small margin of freedom but still enough space to stay alive in? They talked as if they had some helpless stake in American foreign policy, in Britain's negotiations with the common market. Canada for them seemed not so much a sanctuary for individual choice as a place of no choice at all: the dunce cap of the brutal and brutalized country to the south. Paul did not want to defend the United States or Britain; he had precisely enjoyed the freedom not to while he lived in those countries. But he had not come home to feel victimized either by political apathy, the tasteless comfort of new furniture, a renovated childhood. He had come home to build. . . or not. To feel free.

Instead he felt cheated, and, because he was given no opportunity to be directly angry, he began to be subversive, daydreaming aloud about buying an island, retiring before his work began. He'd stop by his friends' houses in the afternoon, wistful and ironic, to discover discontent in their wives. He told sensitive, slightly amused stories about himself.

"I'm not much attached to things," he said, "but when I was writing my thesis and drinking a lot to keep myself company, I discovered a kind of whiskey called *Old Rocking Chair.* Because I bought a lot of it at the same corner store, the owner said one day, 'Wait a minute. I've got something for you.' It was one of those special Christmas bottles he'd saved, I don't know why. I bought it and took it home. When I put it out on the table, I thought I must have set it down on something; it was so unsteady. Then I realized that it had a curved base, and there was a little sign around its neck. It said, 'Touch me. I rock.'"

That was really his best story, if he measured by results: but he did not feel either revenged or free in other people's queen-sized beds. He was disgusted and then bored. Surely not everyone had sold out. There must be somewhere in the city where people played better games or no games at all. The day he was asked to 'design' a knotty pine family room in return for privileges enjoyed, he began to feel desperate.

Why wasn't George still there? Surely he — the kid who had painted his ceiling black and grown poppy seeds before he was twelve — would not have shut himself up in a suburban box with a hair dresser's dummy. When Paul asked about him, he didn't get much information.

"No, George has been in the east for a couple of years. I don't know what he's doing. Said he was going to give up law, but didn't say what for. We didn't see much of him after we all graduated. He had a little house in a back alley behind those beach apartments and was living with a girl. You know how George was. He got moodier. Maybe he'll come back. I think he kept the house. I heard one of his sisters was living in it a while back. With the girl."

Gone, just gone. But, as Paul grew more and more restless, his need to know about George became urgent. He tried to find a phone number in the book. Would it be Alice or Susan or the youngest one, Jane? None of them was listed, and nobody had mentioned the name of George's girl. Maybe they didn't have a phone. Finally he asked for the address, but no one could remember it. They thought it was just behind Shore Avenue, in that alley, somewhere along the two blocks by that strip of park.

On a Sunday evening, Paul drove down along the beach, not certain of finding the place, even less certain that he would call if he did. He parked on the street at the opening of the alley, which was narrow and dark, cluttered with cars which did not seem so much parked there as left for good in various degrees of disrepair. There were only three houses in the first block, two right together and a third wedged in between two garages which served the apartment blocks in front of them. All three were the same vintage, summer beach cottages forty years ago, slatted and shingled by the people who wanted to live in them for several weeks or a month of each year. Built right on the ground at the alley's edge, they had suffered not only from age but from the building projects around them. In the growing dark, it was hazardous to approach, entrances blocked by old cars, rotten boards and broken glass. The single house was dark, but the other two were obviously occupied. In one the shades were drawn. In the other, once Paul had stepped around a pile of old tires and onto the rotting porch, light bright enough for a stage illuminated a room so obviously belonging to George that Paul could not believe George wouldn't momentarily walk into it.

Nobody but George could have invented a room like that. In one corner by a gas fire and cluttered mantle was an old fashioned barber's or perhaps dentist's chair, which had been painted in circus colors. Next to it, dominating the room, was a cane invalid's cart with a single front wheel, steering handle and crank. On the other side of the fire was a chair as distinctive but unrecognizable to Paul in its function. Its thin arms folded inwards and would have to be opened for someone to sit down. Next to that was a leather upholstered bucket seat, obviously from a vintage car. And on the floor, there was the rusting richness of an oriental carpet Paul remembered from the dining room of the old house. He wanted to laugh and could not for a tightness that was also in his throat. George was still alive.

Paul banged on the thin, uncertainly hinged door, and almost at once a girl emerged from the back part of the house, obviously the kitchen. Paul watched her walk across the room, trying to decide if she could be one of George's sisters. Certainly not Alice or Susan, but Jane he hardly remembered, younger than the others, who kept to herself a lot. How old would she be now? This girl could not be more than twenty-two or three, tall, dressed in cultish objects as tattered and complicated as the carpet over which she walked: one of the cool ones.

"I'm a friend of George's," Paul said to her not unwelcoming but silent face. "An old friend. Somebody told me his sister lived here now."

"That's right," the girl agreed. "Come on in."

Once he actually stepped into George's strange set, Paul had a different sense of it, an uncomfortable sense. If George had been there, wry and slowly articulate, Paul would have found an easy part to play at once. Without him, alone in the room since the girl had gone to get George's sister from the kitchen, Paul began to feel the butt of a bad joke. He stood in the center of the room, confronted by the furniture.

"Sit down," the girl said, returning. "Jane's coming."

He chose the car seat, knowing himself judged by the choice. He should have taken the invalid's cart and enjoyed the mutual mockery, his strong, independent body defiantly comfortable in that mortal promise. But he couldn't. He had too much investment in himself that hadn't yet paid off, and he was nervous. He wanted the driver's control.

"You here from Toronto?" the girl asked.

"No, from New York. I haven't seen George for years. I didn't even know he was in Toronto until somebody told me."

He wanted to ask her her name, though he had no idea what use it would be to him. Was she the girl George had lived with? She was casual enough, unselfconscious, and a bit forlorn, more like an object than a person deserted, as she parted the arms of the unidentifiable chair and accommodated her indifferent body to it.

"He's been gone for two years," the girl said.

"Is he planning to come back?"

"Planning? I don't know."

"What's he doing in Toronto?"

"Different things. He's not much of a letter writer."

"No," Paul agreed and remembered his own disappointment when George had not answered those first Canadian bumpkin letters Paul had written, pages and pages of them, but Paul had learned not to be much of a letter writer himself since then. "Does he own this house?"

"Oh no. But the rent's cheap, and he didn't want to store his stuff; so Jane moved in. I was already here."

And George didn't want to store her either or take her with him. Paul did not know why he felt critical of George at that moment. Surely this girl was not, like the furniture, without a will of her own. She stayed on by choice.

"Hi," Jane said, standing in the doorway.

Paul got up to greet her, amazed that he had thought he could not remember her. She had grown up, of course, but there was that same long, dust pale hair so fine it slipped against any restraint so that she had to hold it away from her eyes, a gesture that made her seem always to be looking into the light with wide open, unprotected gaze. She wore no make up, and the planes of her face were still as softly defined as in childhood.

"I would have known you anywhere," Paul said. "I don't suppose you remember me."

"Paul," she said.

"That's right."

"Are you an architect now?"

"I have my ticket," Paul said, glad finally to apologize.

"George got his ticket, too," Jane said. "I suppose you know."

"I heard."

"Buying tickets is all right," the other girl offered, "as long as you don't let yourself get taken for the ride."

"I think so," Paul said, knowing that must be a quotation from George. "That's how I hope I have it figured out."

Jane crossed the room and climbed into the invalid's cart. It was too large for her, and her face was partially hidden by the crank. With her elbows resting on the arms, her hands up to support her hair, she looked somehow crippled, a spastic or someone suffering from deteriorating arthritis. Paul wanted her out of that cart at once. It was not a good joke at all.

"There must be some home brew, Esther," she said. "It's not bad, really."

"Fine," Paul agreed, wishing Jane would go for it, but she did not. "What kinds of things are you doing?" he asked her, looking directly at her, trying to cancel the effect of the cart.

"Art school this year, I guess," Jane said. "Maybe I'll do some teaching at the free school, if the kids want me to."

"You didn't go to the university?"

She smiled at him, and he remembered that, too, slightly derisive as it always had been. "I went."

He decided to stop asking questions. "I took a four year course in eight years. Only way I could stand it."

"And now it's not your thing?"

"I don't know. I thought coming back. . ." But knowing what he knew now, he didn't know how to finish that used up explanation. "I wanted to talk to George, for one thing."

Esther brought in the beer, cidery and so active it resisted swallowing.

"George stopped talking," Esther said.

"Why?"

"He just got hostile about words, I guess," Jane said. "A year in a law office can do it."

"Reading the newspaper can do it," Esther said.

"George always had his times of shutting up," Paul said. "He probably shouldn't have gone into law at all."

"He wanted to know how the system worked," Esther said. "Maybe you want to find out how to build a building. Doesn't mean you have to build one."

"No, but the idea keeps occurring to you," Paul said. "What did he decide to do instead?"

"Didn't decide," Jane said, sipping her beer awkwardly. "He figured out he didn't have to decide."

"Are you waiting for him to come back?" Paul asked both of them.

Jane didn't answer.

"Not exactly," Esther said.

"Did Jimmy bring back the Vivaldi, Esther?" Jane asked. "Do you want to hear Vivaldi?"

Again Jane didn't move. Esther found the record and put it on, but it was not necessary to listen to it carefully, only to rest with it between the intervals of awkward, testing conversation. Paul had a second glass of beer, wishing for something stronger. Next time he'd bring a bottle. He was sure he would come back though he was uncomfortable, even resentful of their basic indifference to him — not to him so much as to what seemed to him important to find out.

"Could you give up this house?" he asked at one point.

"I guess so," Jane answered.

Paul wasn't sure why he had asked the question or what answer he had expected. They must simply be waiting for George. They couldn't give up the house in the normal way of moving because they didn't seem to live there. It was a stage set, and they weren't even actors. Oh, Esther moved around, getting things, doing things, but whatever she put her hands on seemed something she had come across with faint surprise. And Jane looked a cripple in that cart, behaved like one in never moving, but it wasn't her size. Besides, it was meant for the street. She was parked there to be unlikely and then had forgotten the joke of it.

Paul wanted her to talk to him about George, or, if not about George, about herself, but it was Esther who was more willing.

"He was a cook for a while. He bought a motorcycle."

Neither of these facts made sense to Paul. That is, they didn't seem important one way or another.

"What made him decide to go east?"

"You have a decision hang up," Jane said. "Who needs to decide?"

"When he couldn't get a second-hand electric chair for the living room, his work in the west was done," Esther said.

"That would have been a worse joke than the cart. Do you always sit there, Jane?"

"It's not a joke," Jane said. "He had a good idea for a coffee table, too, but it cost too much. It was a woman's laboring bench, stirrups and all."

"It's got to be a sort of joke," Paul protested.

"Why do you sit in the driver's seat?" Esther asked. "As a joke?"

"I didn't want a hair cut or a tooth pulled. I'm not a cripple. I didn't know how to work the thing you're sitting in. I didn't know what it was for."

"We don't either," Esther said. "George thought there ought to be a what-the-hell-is-it-for chair, and I thought I probably ought to sit in it, most of the time."

"And you like to play cripple?" Paul asked Jane.

She shrugged.

"You can buy lots of chairs," Paul said, "but you don't have to sit in them."

"That's what George thought," Esther said.

"But he left you with them, stuck with them. How does that figure?"

"It's a place," Esther said. "It's cheap. It's true enough."

But George wouldn't live in it — because he couldn't find a retired American electric chair? because he couldn't afford a laboring bench? because he couldn't stand how true it was? because Esther didn't really know how to live in it with him?

"Get out of that damned thing," Paul said to Jane.

"I'm not afraid of it. You have to get used to it. . . or not."

He accepted that. He didn't seem to have a choice. The beer was sour in his stomach. Esther yawned. Paul hadn't told any of his sensitive, slightly amused stories. Next time. From the barber's chair, or was it a dentist's chair? From the cart so Jane couldn't sit in it. If he did come back.

Paul walked back through the dark alley and drove home, thinking of George, thinking of their boyhood together, when they sat on rocks and bicycle seats and the roof outside George's bedroom window. He climbed the stairs to his own bedroom, unchanged but for a new coat of paint since he'd left it eight years before. There had never been much in it; some books, a painting he had bought in an undergraduate phase to impress himself. It was true he never much attached to things. But there was the bottle on his dresser.

"Touch me. I rock."

Housekeeper

None of her friends could understand how Ruth Tedmore, an extremely competent personnel manager of a large department store, could hire, year after year, such catastrophically bad help for her own household. Ruth, on the other hand, understood it perfectly and painfully well. But it was clearly against her interests to explain herself.

Ruth had the only kind of job she seemed good at, making intelligent and perceptive decisions for other people. Her quick eye for spotting trouble on an application form was only the beginning. Once she had eliminated the bad risks, she did not look for perfection or even excellence, nor did she pay very much attention to either interest or aptitude. If she had, her days would have been full of dull disappointments. What Ruth looked for was a fault that the manager or assistant manager of a particular department could not only endure but perhaps even, in a perverse way, enjoy. What she tried to avoid was virtue which would irritate or threaten. Ruth did not think of herself as cynical so much as realistic. The most efficient and talented salesman cannot last more than a month under a threatened manager.

The store did not pay enough to hire many managers who could tolerate talent; on the other hand, the clerks' salaries were discouraging enough to attract very few problems of that sort. Skillful fault-matching was Ruth's forte. Its success, however, depended on the ignorance of the people who benefited from it. Mr. Lambert, in yard goods, could never be told that he liked stupidity in his clerks; yet he pined in the stock room unless his advice was needed for almost every sale. Mrs. Caldwell in foundation garments needed an assertive vulgarity in her clerks so that she never had to come out of the stock room. Ruth knew all her managers and assistant managers well. Over the years, she had been careful with their variety so that there was some place in the store for the impudent, the slovenly, the complaining, the nervous, whose virtues might also, if they were lucky, be tolerated.

Because the store, under Ruth Tedmore's direction, had a remarkable record for permanence of staff, she had several times been asked to offer training programs for personnel managers both in the store itself for its other branches and in the local business college. Ruth had always refused. She knew that her skill, once confessed, would neither appeal to students nor reassure those who already lived in terms of it. The store would come down around her ears.

It was as impossible to explain to her baffled friends how she came to have such remarkably bad housekeepers. Fortunately she had never been pressed to explain the failure of her marriage. As for her children, she had not been able to choose those, an important advantage in her law of averages.

"Ruth," her next door neighbor had just confided, "it just doesn't seem fair for you to have such bad luck, but you really ought to know that this one doesn't do any more work than the last. She was out in the back yard yesterday for five hours, drinking beer. Did she have references? Most people from the good agencies are checked out for things like that."

Ruth had never used a good agency, and she probably never would. Most of the help she had came from her rejects at the store, women eliminated on first glance at the application form because they were, in one way or another, blatantly unreliable: divorcees with small children, wives of construction workers, foreigners, college graduates. What made them unsuitable as clerks in a store made them as unsuitable as housekeepers: they had too many distracting responsibilities and griefs; they were transient; they were strange in their habits; they were intelligent.

"I don't want a permanent, motherly soul who knows how to scrub a kitchen floor," Ruth might have said, for that was true; she did not want to compete with such virtues. Or she might have tried to comfort her tale-bearing friends with, "Tell me more; every terrible story is a reassurance to me."

Just as the store would come down around Ruth's ears if her managers had known how they were being handled, Ruth's house again and again did come down around her ears because she could not help knowing what she was doing to herself.

Anna Wilmott, her current beer-drinking beauty, was even more a hazard and mistake than Ruth had anticipated. Anna, too well dressed and confident of her offense, had sat amused in Ruth's office while she reread the application form, knowing that she should not have granted Anna an interview in the first place.

"I see you've been to college," Ruth said cautiously.

"Well, but I'm a drop out," Anna answered reassuringly.

"You've had a number of jobs."

"I get bored."

"You're married with three children."

"So far, but, if I can stick with this job for a year, I can save enough money to get out."

"Leave your husband?"

"That's the plan."

"And the children?"

"He thinks I won't take them. It all depends . . ."

"You haven't given a preference for the kind of job you'd like to do."

"I didn't see any place on the form for drinking or mountain climbing."

"You don't really want this job, do you?" Ruth asked, without irritation.

"Does anybody really want a job in a place like this?"

"Let me put it another way: you don't really need the job."

"Oh yes I do," Anna said with sudden intensity. "My life depends on it."

Ruth hadn't hired her, of course, but she remembered Anna Wilmott for several reasons. She was remarkably good looking with fine, shining hair, large, dark eyes, an expression much gentler than the manner she affected. Her body was not vulgar, but it promised things naturally as a bright day promises warmth, pleasure. And Anna, though she had been aggressive, had hoped to win rather than alienate Ruth with directness. Anna's last remark had been effective, whether calculated as emotional blackmail or not. Ruth might have said the same thing when she was first interviewed for a job at the store if she hadn't had more calculating sense than that.

They did not meet again by appointment. Ruth had reluctantly given in to Sunday on the beach with her children, Jennifer, who was eight, and Tad, not quite six. Ruth didn't like the beach because it was too warm for the clothes she was willing to wear in public, because the children forced her into domestic conversations with other mothers. Still, it eased her guilt to do something she didn't like with her children during the little time she spent with them. Jennifer had learned to swim that summer; that is, she could thrash and splash enough to keep her feet off the bottom for a moment or two at a time. Tad was still really suspicious of the water. Nothing he found washed up on the beach was beneath his curiosity, but those same things floating in the water touched his imagination differently. While Jennifer plunged and sputtered, he collected and built at the edge of Ruth's grass mat. She watched in resigned, sticky, gritty discomfort from behind her sun glasses and large straw hat.

In that disguise, Ruth might have seen and then watched Anna without encountering her again. She was in a yellow bikini, playing roughly with two little boys, one a little younger and one a little older than Tad. The younger complained about the game, stamped out of the water and stood at the edge, yelling obscenities of such variety at his mother that only the adults within earshot were impressed. Anna ignored him until he wore himself out and threw himself down on the sand. Then she scooped him up suddenly to kiss or perhaps bite his ear. He pulled her hair, kissed her and scrambled free, laughing. Tad, at the shore line, had stopped his search for objects and was watching with the stunned stare of a child for any behavior he finds bewildering. Anna, giving up her chase of her own child just as she neared Tad, spoke to him. Ruth expected him to retreat, but in a moment he was showing Anna a rusted light socket and a small piece of wood. The older son, a couple of inches taller than Tad, had joined them. Just then, Jennifer started out of the water with a new friend, a tall, angular, light-boned girl of perhaps nine. They joined Anna and the boys for a moment.

"Mom, can we have hot dogs? Sally's mother says they can," Jennifer called as she came up the sloping beach to her mother.

Anna turned to look at Ruth, probably not recognizing her, but Ruth did not want to risk rudeness.

"Hello," she called.

Anna walked up toward her, the children in her wake, and Ruth noticed the quizzical sweetness of her face.

"I'm Ruth Tedmore from. . ."

"I didn't recognize you in that get up," Anna said. "If I had, I would have run away."

"Why?"

"People like you scare me," Anna said, dropping down on the straw mat next to Ruth. "Now, out, the pack of you. Sally, you get the money from my purse."

"What about us?" Jennifer demanded.

"All right," Ruth said. "Be sure Tad doesn't get relish on his by mistake."

"And be sure you bring us back some," Anna added. "I'm starved."

Ruth could say, therefore, that the whole arrangement was an accident. There were also real advantages. The children liked Anna, her combination of boisterous, rough affection and mindless indifference to them. More important, they all liked each other, absorbed each other for hours at a time, and, because Anna ignored their hostilities (more for her own peace than for their good), they fought very little when they were all together.

"But, Ruth, how many times a week does she leave one of those kids with you? You do as much baby sitting for her as she does for you. Only she gets paid for it."

But that wasn't a real problem. Honestly, the children were less trouble together than apart, the girls off in

Jennifer's room writing novels or cutting out free coupons from magazines, the boys on the living room floor dreaming over and crashing their cars into each other when the television program wasn't interesting enough for them. If Anna decided to go home without one or more of her own children, she always cooked enough dinner for all of them before she left. She didn't spend more than Ruth gave her for food; she just bought cheaper cuts to accommodate more people. Ruth's children, as well as Anna's, liked hot dogs and hamburgers and spaghetti best anyway. Ruth got pretty tired of such fare, but she could have a decent, adult lunch at work.

Jennifer was no more affected by Anna's graphic vocabulary than her own daughter was. They were at a very moral, even prissy age. Tad, on the other hand, competed with his new friends in foul-mouthed joy. He could have learned the same thing at school, no doubt; and after all, he was a boy. If he'd had a father, his vocabulary wouldn't have been retarded for so long. Actually, the husband who had left Ruth would never have used such language. She was thinking of the kind of man she might have married if she had been someone else.

Anna certainly did drink beer or wine or gin or whiskey, anything Ruth left in the house. When Ruth stopped leaving it or hid it, Anna obviously got cheaper wines out of the household budget. In fact, she once or twice admitted to such a purchase, or rather announced it. She never got really drunk, but often she had a kind of blurred amusement about her, and she would have broken and spilled and gouged more if she had spent more time at the cleaning up she was also hired to do.

"Couldn't face the dishes today," she'd often say. "Just leave the whole bunch for the morning."

117

Ruth had a lot of china and glassware because she had pass those counters every day, but, when she was reduced to stemware and Wedgewood for the children's supper, she did the dishes herself and was resentful.

As for house cleaning, even Ruth's own shamefully low standards were not observed. A month went by before Ruth ordered Anna to clean the children's rooms and wash the kitchen floor. For such things as washing windows and defrosting the refrigerator, even orders were useless. Anna simply did not include such activities within the range of her comprehension. Her method was to ignore a job until Ruth's temper finally flared. Then Anna would say, "Get yourself a slave if that's what you want."

Ruth didn't want a slave. She didn't even want a competent housekeeper, but surely between these ideals and Anna, there must be a more rational compromise. Ruth would not even have to fire Anna. She offered to quit every five or six days. The children would miss each other, of course, and they'd miss the freedom since Anna obviously found it easier to discover them after the damage was done than before they had thought of it; but a little more discipline would do neither of them any harm. Anna herself, as the months passed, talked less and less about leaving her husband. She didn't need the money for anything else certainly, though Ruth had never found out what Anna's husband did. Once she asked outright.

"God knows," was Anna's reply.

She had an unnervingly good address, drove an expensive car, and she and her children were well, if sometimes oddly, dressed.

Why, then, as Ruth's friends more persistently asked, did she put up with Anna?

"Because I'd rather nag than be nagged."

"Because I didn't put up with my husband, and I feel guilty about it."

"Because I don't have to compete."

Those were the reasons, and they would have been fine reasons if Ruth hadn't known about them. Knowing about them made the relationship intolerable, as all her relationships with housekeepers had been. In the past, after a number of punishing months, everything had collapsed, just as her marriage had collapsed around the faults she had needed and knew she needed in her husband. Why did she have to know? Why couldn't she be the innocent victim of her own temperament as all her managers and assistant managers had been for years? Because she couldn't. Part of her nature was to know. So Ruth prepared for finding intolerable what really suited her relatively well.

The crisis did not come. Imperceptibly the tension lessened. Ruth was both baffled and relieved. It was not that Anna worked any harder or drank less, but she occasionally baked pies or worked in the garden, and once, when Ruth got home, the old arm chair in the living room was draped with a handsome piece of material.

"If you like that, I'll recover it for you," Anna said.

"I like it very much. How much is it?"

Anna shrugged.

"But I should pay you for it."

"Why? I cheat you every day; so I should be able to treat you once in six months."

"You don't cheat me . . . " Ruth began, but the amusement in those large, dark eyes stopped her. "Well, thanks."

Then Anna, contrite about her generosity, left at least two of her children behind every night for the next week. Ruth, instead of being irritated, was amused.

"That chair was pretty expensive after all," she said to Anna.

"I wouldn't want you to feel guilty about it," Anna said.

That night, sitting in the chair Anna had recovered, Ruth saw the name, Charles Wilmott, in the paper under a photograph of a fine-jawed, quiet-eyed man, unmistakably father of Sally, therefore Anna's husband. His appointment as director of a large company was being announced. As Ruth read a summary of his career, she felt the twinge of envy she always had for men capable of such success and free, because they were men, to enjoy it. Almost immediately she felt ashamed and then alarmed, for suddenly Anna Wilmott, incompetent housekeeper, became Mrs. Charles Wilmott, wife to this competent man. Surely he must know. Why would he allow it? Anna must have threatened him. Or perhaps having her busy, whatever she did, was preferable to having her unhappily at home. Why would a man like Charles Wilmott want such a wife? Why wouldn't he simply let her leave? The children. Ruth looked again at his face, a good face, a little complacent perhaps, but vulnerable. One of the several sorts of men Ruth would never have dared to marry, if she'd been given the opportunity. Anna had dared. Ruth understood how she could, for Anna had no intention of living up to anyone, threatening anyone. Cheat she certainly did and take advantage of and disappoint in a dozen ways a day, but she never threatened anyone else's self esteem. Thinking of Anna, Ruth was suddenly very afraid of losing her. She got up, went to the kitchen and started to defrost the refrigerator. Perhaps, if she didn't mention the newspaper article, Anna wouldn't either.

In the morning, because Anna was more than usually late, there wasn't time for any conversation at all, but, when

Ruth got home that night, she entered the house with depressed apprehension.

"We made a hole in the ceiling," Tad announced with his relatively new confidence in brazening things out. "With water."

"They let the tub run over," Jennifer explained, prissy with innocence.

"Where's Anna?"

"Taking a nap."

Ruth found her sound asleep on the living room couch.

"Wake up, Anna!" she commanded with a free anger. "Wake up!"

Anna smiled, but that sweetness could not touch Ruth. The expense of her drinking was one thing; finding her in an alcoholic stupor while the ceiling literally caved in was another.

"You're fired," Ruth said the moment Anna opened those dark, appealing, faintly amused eyes. "Now, this minute."

"I'll have to come back tomorrow and fix that ceiling," Anna said, rubbing her face as if it hurt. "You didn't have any plaster."

"You're not setting foot in this house again," Ruth said, her voice under control for the sake of the children, clustered and silent in the doorway.

"We can't come back anyway," Sally announced, defensive. "Daddy won't let us."

"Pack it up, Sally," Anna said.

"He said . . ." one of the boys began.

"Out, all of you," Anna ordered with the rare authority they always obeyed.

"So I'm fired," Anna said, once the children were gone, 'and I quit."

"You simply haven't any sense of responsibility," Ruth said, trying to maintain an anger that was draining away as fast as it had come.

"I know."

"I've been willing to put up with a lot."

"I know."

"What if one of the children had been hurt? What if there'd been a fire?" But as Ruth proposed these catastrophes, not only they but the scene she was making seemed increasingly unreal. "Why did you do it?"

"You know perfectly well why I did it," Anna said with weary impatience. "I have to quit. You might as well know how little you're losing."

"That's stupid."

"Of course it is. But how else can you feel right about it? How else can I? That was a really good job you did on the refrigerator, you know? You might even be able to stand somebody who could clean a house and liked to."

"And what virtues do you think I've taught you?" Ruth asked sarcastically.

"None," Anna said, helping herself to one of Ruth's cigarettes. "Except I saw you knew what you were doing, and that made me think maybe Charlie knew what he was doing, too, and didn't like it any better than you do."

"What good does it do to know?" Ruth demanded, her role as righteous employer gone. "If I can't stop?"

"I don't know. Who wants to be perfect anyway?"

"I do," Ruth said.

Anna offered again one of her quizzical, uncritical smiles, full of moral indifference and pleasure. "I like you the way you are. It's not a bad game to play once you know the way it works."

"That's not true," Ruth said. "Knowing how it works ruins it."

"Silly hole in the ceiling. Silly hangover," Anna said and laughed. "Anyway, I am coming back to fix it in the morning. You'll just have to risk the house burning down."

"But then you can't come any more?"

"No."

"What am I going to do?"

"Phone an agency," Anna said, echoing the years of advice of all Ruth's responsible friends but adding, with a knowledge they didn't have, "You don't have to be afraid. The housekeeper I've got isn't all that much better than I am, and she's recommended."

"Why on earth did you take the job?"

"I told you: my life depended on it."

"And now it doesn't?"

"I hope not," Anna said.

Ruth sat in her office, her hand on the phone, thinking of Anna plastering up the hole in the ceiling before she went home to be a wife to Charlie, who needed her more than Ruth did. Or had the right to her. Did he really know as well as Ruth did how much his self esteem depended on someone else always being wrong? She dialed.

"A motherly person," she said, "who can scrub a kitchen floor and defrost a refrigerator."

After all, nobody was perfect. Anybody she hired was bound to have a small fault or two for her to fall back on. But Ruth saw Anna's large, dark, amused eyes, and she felt bereft as she had only once before in her life.

If There
Is No Gate

Once before, when I was twenty, I thought I was losing my mind. Then, too, I'd been working hard, and I suppose I'd caught a touch of paranoia as one does a cold in the early spring, when there's a sudden thaw and a temporary aggression of crocuses. One feels unprepared, put upon. I don't remember just what it was, an excess of defensive energy, ill temper, loneliness. I only remember the fear, like a blown fuse in the nervous system, a darkness in the heart. I was driving out to the mental hospital to deliver a load of clothes and books my mother had collected from the neighborhood. She spent all her time, and a good deal of mine, collecting comfort for distant, public catastrophes. It was her way of protecting herself and her family from the fraud of any private terror. We had no time for such nonsense. It was a compliment that she had allowed me to go, the first of her children to reach the age of immunity. She was a marvelously insensitive woman.

My old school uniform, neatly folded just as it had been in the bottom drawer of my dresser, was at the top of the box, an afterthought smelling faintly of camphor. I lifted the carton out of the trunk of the car and, following the signs marked OFFICE, carried it through the archway into the inner court. I had not intended to look around. I had intended to keep my eyes fixed on that shroud of my innocence, my anonymity, like a charmed relic of another life, but all about and above me the racket of cries startled me into the world. There behind great expanses of steel mesh, level upon level storying up against the light, were trapped covies of women, shrieking and calling like surprised birds. It was a gigantic aviary of madness. Some wailed, high and fierce, unmated in that limited and crowded sky. Others chattered and scolded to guard some memory of a shabby nest, of frail and greedy young. A few hopped mournfully, silently about, picking at scraps. There were pairs, too, bold and impersonal as doves under the eaves. One woman, holding another, rocked and sang a vacant lullaby, as pure as any bird song, as inhuman. I walked across the court, went into the office, and delivered the box. I was glad to walk back through that court, empty-handed.

Sometimes since then, when I have been disturbed at dawn by the distant, violent wings of geese or at dusk by the pedestrian entrance of a robin, I have used that human aviary as a touchstone of sanity. It has been for me one of the unnatural wonders of the world, like a great cathedral, a sanctuary where one can take all the fears of one's inhumanity, leave them at the feet of saints, and come away at peace.

But that day seems a long way back in my memory, in feeling vaguer than more recent prayers. It is hard to recall not the scene so much as the sense of it: the exact, unspectacular relief of being an intentional, inhibited, insensitive human being. Perhaps the experience no longer becomes me, fits too smugly over my middle-aged humility, like a confirmation dress or a wedding gown. But, if that is so, then sanity itself must be a convention one can outgrow. One can, but one mustn't. Surely recovery, not discovery, is the way back to health.

Here they do not want me to recall the particulars of my life, to retrace my steps until I find the place, the precise moment of error. I am to ignore my conscious memory and the ordering power of my brain, as if moral interpretation of experience were a disease to be cured of. Instead, I am to enter the world of dreams and visions, abandon myself to the freakish chaos of a night's sleep, awake clinging to the absurdities and obscenities out of Spiritus Mundi and talk or dance or paint them all the unordinary day long.

If I were in a cage, dressed in someone else's clothes, absent-minded, it would be so much simpler to be mad, but this is not a mental hospital. It is a kind of rest home, settled against the gentle Devon hills within taste of the sea. I have my own small room under the eaves, sunny, vines friendly at the window, like a picture in a children's book of poetry. I am free to do what I like, to go where I please, even out into the little village to buy fruit or a bottle of sherry. I wash out my own underthings, sew on buttons, send my clothes to the cleaner. And my mind, untouched by the sudden willess attacks of fear that my body suffers, is more decorous and lucid than ever. I make polite, intelligent conversation with the doctors at afternoon tea in the garden. My own doctor, a woman of huge frame with a face warm and remote as the sun, was once a 'guest' here. She had gone from psychiatry to a silent order only to find, after five years, that it was not her vocation. It is peculiarly easy to talk to one in whom silence has lived so deeply. But it is peculiarly easy to talk to everyone here, guests and doctors. One simply learns to be mannerly in the presence of visions. If I come upon a girl dancing naked by the little stream that crosses the southwest corner of the property, I simply turn my eyes away to watch the gardener clipping the hedge or the swans copulating fiercely, awkwardly in the late afternoon sun. If I sit on a bench next to a boy who is sticking pins into the clay image of his father, I go on with my mending. But I am still, after all these weeks, appalled. I cannot and do not wish to dance naked in the sun. I loathe fine bits of clay which circle my nails and mute the lines in my palms. I haven't the skill to paint what I have seen awake or dreaming, and, if I can be taught to value nightmares, I cannot be taught to value my own crude approximations of them. I am still trapped in the hope of real articularity.

When I first came here, in a daze of sedatives, I could not dream at all. I fell into sleep like a stone into water, settling deep and undisturbed in the darkness. Only when I was awake was I victim to sudden, unreasoning fears, fits of trembling exhaustion. I was willing then to talk, afraid as I was to make the journey back through the years alone, no longer trusting my own memory. But I agreed that it could not be grief or shame that had driven me here. The first I suffered when the only child I could have was born dead. I was so brave, so dull, that my husband finally took his weight of sympathy and tenderness to someone else, someone who needed him. The shame I found bearable, too, first in anger, then in resignation. My husband is a nervous, high-spirited, good-looking man with a flare for misery. I have none. I agreed, too, that it is something vaguer, deeper than these very personal, very limited experiences that challenges stability — or maintains it. And so I went where the doctor took me, gradually allowing myself to be taught to dream, then more slowly to admit the dream into the waking world.

I did not find the new habit hard to form, and for a while dreams did seem to replace memory. The first were not difficult to understand, perhaps because I could relate them to what had actually happened. I stood on a great raft in a violent sea. All around me friends drank cocktails and chatted, unaware of danger for themselves or of the desperate struggle I was involved in. I saw my dying child in the sea, in its face my own, as if I looked from its eyes and yet felt my fear. I threw a rope, but suddenly my husband was drowning, and, each time I tried to pull him aboard the raft, I found myself dragged nearer the edge. That loved face, out of whose eyes I could now see my own life threatened. I was lying on an operating table, asking for a doctor. The psychiatrist, in the habit of a nun, looked down at me and said, "You know your child is dead." Yes, I know. I have always known that. Then I was much younger, pleading with my mother. I did not want to walk up to a strange house, ring the doorbell, and ask for donations of eyes, arms, teeth, genitals. Mother opened a suitcase to show me what she had already collected. The eyes were only painted eggs, the arms and legs the broken pieces of my own china dolls. Then I saw a row of decaying teeth, hooked loosely into bone. Rain fell, peacefully, peacefully, on shells, on sand, and my child slept among starfish and seaweed, rocking in the receding tide.

I did not mind recording those dreams; I had some conscious knowledge of each image, and gradually I recovered that old skill of sifting the simple facts from the irrelevant desires. The unconscious once recognized, however, will not continue to accommodate the moral intellect with fables.

What was I to do with the dream of myself soaking my husband's raincoat in the car radiator, then cutting it into strips and frying it for his breakfast? What was I to do with rules like "Change I to you and add e-s" which I seemed to be teaching to strange natives? One night I dreamt of a gangster standing in the road, having his portrait painted by dozen middle-aged women while he made a speech about the evils of suicide. He carried and waved two old frontier pistols to illustrate his talk, then suddenly dropped dead, his hair changing from black to red as he lay in the dust.

What shape could I make, standing in the studio before the canvas? The woman next to me was painting a series of pictures in which a crab slowly crawls from the surface of the earth to the center, curls and flowers into a mating couple. What power she was in touch with I do not know as the mindless accuracy of her hand traced each new meaning. No power prompted me to paint strips of frying raincoat, a comic gangster.

I left the studio this morning for an appointment with my doctor. As I turned into the walk, my way was blocked by a young boy. He stood, exposing himself to a bird, a flower, or me. I could not tell. As the bird rose up, I felt one violent shudder of wings in my own passive womb, then the familiar, terrible vacancy. I did not hurry past him. There was no need. I walked as quietly as I have always walked down the path to the house.

"I did not dream it," I said to the doctor. "I saw it. If only they were my own dreams: I have seen spastic children cover their distorted faces with Hallowe'en masks in order to frighten their mothers. I have seen African tribal dancers chase imaginary lions through Windsor Great Park. I have seen two women, dressed for a party, wrestling in a row boat in the middle of the Serpentine."

She did not answer.

"I wish you could understand me."

I waited in her silence, thinking in her silence. It is not the unconscious world of my own nightmares where I find visions. I have never neglected the beached treasures and horrors of my own life. I know they are there, not to be collected and studied and saved, but to be left where they are as part of the natural landscape of the soul. It is not the child washing in the tide, the husband gone, the hopes cut adrift that have wrecked me on my own shore.

"It's the world outside myself and my control, the public catastrophes I cannot be held responsible for. It's other people's nightmares that live in my back garden."

Still she did not speak.

"I can't go mad. I've tried. I have no vocation."

"Nothing keeps you here," she finally answered. "There are no walls. There is no gate."

My suitcase is open on the bed, my clothes neatly packed. As I stand here, waiting for the taxi to come, I can look down, through any one of the dozen small panes of the window, into the garden. There they all are in the ritual of afternoon tea. In the coming and going from the table, in the passing of cups, in the gathering and separating, it is rather like a dance, patterned and yet casual. There is the boy I encountered this morning, sitting quietly in the sun over by the stream. There is my painting companion, talking with the doctor. Now people begin to drift away, free in the garden, free in the world, a huge sky overhead, disturbed only occasionally by a cloud or a line of jet vapor droppings. It is I who am closed away in this small room under the eaves. If there are no walls, if there is no gate, I should like to have asked that huge-framed silent woman not what kept me in but what kept me out; but I should think, like me, she does not know.

Middle Children

Clare and I both come from big families, a bossy, loving line of voices stretching away above us to the final authority of our parents, a chorus of squawling, needy voices beneath us coming from crib or play pen or notch in tree. We share, therefore, the middle child syndrome: we are both over earnest, independent, inclined to claustrophobia in crowds. The dreams of our adolescent friends for babies and homes of their own we privately considered nightmares. Boys were irredeemably brothers who took up more physical and psychic space than was ever fair. Clare and I, in cities across the continent from each other, had the same dream: scholarships for college where we would have single rooms, jobs after that with our own apartments. But scholarship students aren't given single rooms; and the matchmakers, following that old cliche that opposites attract, put us, east and west, into the same room.

Without needing to discuss the matter, we immediately arranged the furniture as we had arranged furniture with sisters all our lives, mine along one wall, hers along the other, an invisible line drawn down the center of the room, over which no sock or book or tennis racket should ever stray. Each expected the other to be hopelessly untidy; our sisters were. By the end of the first week, ours was the only room on the corridor that looked like a military barracks. Neither of us really liked it, used to the posters and rotting corsages and dirty clothes of our siblings, but neither of us could bring herself to contribute any clutter of her own. "Maybe a painting?" Clare suggested. I did not know where we could get one. Clare turned out to be a painter. I, a botanist, who could never grow things in my own room before where they might be watered with coke or broken by a thrown magazine or sweater, brought in a plant stand, the first object to straddle the line because it needed to be under the window. The friends each of us made began to straddle that line, too, since we seemed to be interchangeably good listeners, attracting the same sort of flamboyant, needy first or last or only children.

"Sandra thinks she may be pregnant," I would say about Clare's friend who had told me simply because Clare wasn't around.

"Aren't they all hopeless?" Clare would reply, and we middle children would shake our wise, cautious heads.

We attracted the same brotherly boys as well who took us to football games and fraternity drunks and sexual wrestling matches on the beach. We used the same cool defenses, gleaned not from the advice of our brothers but from observing their behaviour.

"Bobby always told me not to take the 'respect' bit too seriously if I wanted to have any fun," Clare said, "but I sometimes wonder why I'd want 'respect' or 'fun'. Doesn't it all seem to you too much trouble? This Saturday there's a marvelous exhibit. Then we could just go out to dinner and come home."

We had moved our desks by then. Shoved together, they could share one set of reference books conveniently and frugally for us both. We asked to have one chest of drawers taken out of the room. Neither of us had many clothes, and, since we wore the same size, we had begun to share our underwear and blouses to keep laundry day to once a week. I can't remember what excuse we had for moving the beds. Perhaps by the time we did, we didn't need an excuse, for ourselves anyway.

I have often felt sorry for people who can't have the experience of falling in love like that, gradually, without knowing it, touching first because pearls have to be fastened or a collar straightened, then more casually because you are standing close together looking at the same assignment sheet or photograph, then more purposefully because you know that there is comfort and reassurance for an exam coming up or trouble in the family. So many people reach out to each other before there is any sympathy or affection. When Clare turned into my arms, or I into hers — neither of us knows just how it was — the surprise was like coming upon the right answer to a question we did not even know we had asked.

Through the years of college, while our friends suffered all the uncertainties of sexual encounter, of falling into and out of love, of being too young and then perhaps too old in a matter of months, of worrying about how to finance graduate school marriages, our only problem was the clutter of theirs. We would have liked to clear all of them out earlier in order to enjoy the brief domestic sweetness of our own sexual life. But we were from large families. We knew how to maintain privacy, a space of our own, so tactfully that no one ever noticed it. Our longing for our own apartment, like the trips we would take to Europe, was an easy game. Nothing important to us had to be put off until then.

Putting off what was unimportant sometimes did take ingenuity. The boys had no objection to being given up, but our corridor friends were continually trying to arrange dates for us. We decided to come back from one Christmas holiday engaged to boys back home. That they didn't exist was never discovered. We gave each other rings and photographs of brothers. Actually I was very fond of Bobby, and Clare got on just as well with my large and boisterous family. Our first trip to Europe, between college and graduate school, taught us harder lessons. It seemed harmless enough to drink and dance with the football team traveling with us on the ship, but, when they turned up, drunken and disorderly at our London hotel, none of our own outrage would convince the night porter that we were not at fault. Only when we got to graduate school did we find the social answer: two young men as in need of protection as we were, who cared about paintings and concerts and growing things and going home to their own bed as much as we did.

When Clare was appointed assistant professor in art history and I got a job with the parks board, we had been living together in dormitories and student digs for eight years. We could finally leave the clutter of other lives behind us for an apartment of our own. Just at a time when we saw other relationships begin to grow stale or burdened with the continual demands of children, we were discovering the new privacy of making love on our own living room carpet at five o'clock in the afternoon, too hungry then to bother with cocktails or dressing for dinner. Soon we got quite out of the habit of wearing clothes except when we went out or invited people in. We woke making love, ate breakfast and made love again before we went to work, spent three or four long evenings a week in the same new delight until I saw in Clare's face that bruised, ripe look of a new, young wife, and she said at the same moment, "You don't look safe to go out."

In guilt we didn't really discuss, we arranged more evenings with friends, but, used to the casual interruptions of college life, we found such entertainment often too formal and contrived. Then for a week or two we would return to our honeymoon, for alone together we could find no reason not to make love. It is simply not true to say such things don't improve with practice.

"It's a good thing we never knew how bad we were at it," Clare said, one particularly marvelous morning.

When we didn't know, however, we had had more sympathy for those around us, accommodating themselves to back seats of cars or gritty blankets on the beach. Now our friends, either newly wed in student digs where quarreling was the only acceptable — that is, unavoidable — noise, or exhausted by babies, made wry jokes about missing the privacy of drive-in movies or about the merits of longer bathtubs. They were even more avid readers of pornography than they had been in college. We were not the good listeners we had been. I heard Clare being positively high minded about what a waste of time all those dirty books were.

"You never used to be a prude," Sandra said in surprise.

That remark, which should have made Clare laugh, kept her weeping half the night instead. I had never heard her so distressed, but then perhaps she hadn't had the freedom to be. "We're too different," she said, and "We're not kind any more."

"Maybe we should offer to baby sit for Sandra and lend them the apartment," I suggested, not meaning it.

We are both very good with babies. It would be odd if we weren't. Any middle child knows as much about colic and croup as there is to know by the time she's eight or nine.

The initial squeamishness about changing diapers is conquered at about the same age. Sandra, like all our other friends, had it all to learn at twenty-three. Sometimes we did just as I had suggested, sitting primly across from each other like maiden aunts, Clare marking papers, I thumbing through books that could help me to imagine what was going on in our apartment. Or sometimes Sandra would call late at night, saying, "You're fond of this kid, aren't you? Well, come and get him before we kill him." Then we'd take the baby for a midnight ride over the rough back roads that are better for gas pains than any pacing. I didn't mind that assignment, but I was increasingly restless with the evenings we spent in somebody else's house.

"You know, if we had a house of our own," I said, "we could take the baby for the night, and they could just stay home.."

I realize that there is nothing really immoral about lending your apartment to a legally married couple for the evening so that you can spend a kind and moral night out with their baby, but it seemed to me faintly and unpleasantly obscene: our bed . . . perhaps even our living room rug. I was back to the middle child syndrome. I wanted to draw invisible lines.

"They're awfully tidy and considerate," Clare said, "and they always leave us a bottle of scotch."

"Well, we leave them a bottle of scotch as well."

"We drink more of it than they do."

I didn't want to sound mean.

"If we had a house, we could have a garden."

"You'd like that," Clare decided.

Sandra's husband said we could never get a mortgage, but our combined income was simply too impressive to ignore. We didn't really need a large house, just the two of us, though I wanted a studio for Clare, and she wanted a green house and work shop for me. The difficulty was that neither of us could think of a house that was our size. We weren't used to them. The large, old houses that felt like home were really no more expensive than the new, compact and efficient boxes the agent thought suitable to our career centered lives. Once we had wandered through the snarled, old garden and up into the ample rooms of the sort of house we had grown up in, we could not think about anything else.

"Well, why not?" I asked

"It has five bedrooms."

"We don't have to use them all."

"We might take a student," Clare said.

We weren't surprised at the amount of work involved in owning an old house. Middle children aren't. Our friends, most of whom were still cooped up in apartments, liked to come out in those early days for painting and repair parties, which ended with barbecue suppers on the back lawn, fenced in and safe for toddlers. Our current couple of boys were very good at the heavy work of making drapes and curtains. They even enjoyed helping me dig out old raspberry canes. It was two years before Clare had time to paint in the studio, and my green house turned out to be a very modest affair since I had so many other things to do, cooking mostly.

We have only one room left now for stray children. The rest are filled with students, boys we decided, which is probably a bit prudish, and it's quite true that they take up more physical and psychic space than is ever fair. Still, they're only kids, and, though it takes our saintly cleaning woman half a day a week just to dig out their rooms, they're not bad about the rest of the house.

Harry is a real help to me with the wine making, inclined to be more careful about the chemical details than

I am. Pete doesn't leave his room except to eat unless we've got some of the children around; then he's even willing to stay with them in the evening if we have to go out. Carl, who's never slept a night alone in his life since he discovered it wasn't necessary, doesn't change girls so often that we don't get to know them, and he has a knack for finding people who fit in: take a turn at the dishes, walk the dogs, check to see that we have enough cream for breakfast.

Clare and I have drawn one very careful line across the door of our bedroom, and, though it's not as people proof as our brief apartment, it's a good deal better than a dormitory. We even occasionally have what we explain as our cocktail there before dinner when one of Carl's girls is minding the vegetables; and, if we don't get involved in too interesting a political or philosophical discussion, we sometimes go upstairs for what we call the late news. Both of us are still early to wake, and, since Pete will get up with any visiting child, the first of the day is always our own.

"Pete's a middle child," Clare said the other morning, hearing him sing a soft song to Sandra's youngest as he carried her down the stairs to give her an early bottle. "I hope he finds a middle child for himself one day."

"I'd worry about him if he were mine," I said.

"Oh, well, I'd worry about any of them if they were mine. I simply couldn't cope."

"I just wouldn't want to."

"There's a boy in my graduate seminar . ." Clare began.

I was tempted to say that, if we had a family of our own, we'd always be worrying and talking about them even when we had time to ourselves, but there was still an hour before we had to get up, and I've always felt generous in the early morning, even when I was a kid in a house cluttered with kids from which I dreamed that old dream of escape.

140

My Country Wrong

There should always be a reason for going somewhere: a death in the family, a lover, a need for sun, at least a simple curiosity. Even a business trip provides excuse for discomfort, focuses discontent. To explain why I arrived in San Francisco on the twenty-third of December, instead of on the twenty-sixth when I was expected, would be nothing but a list of nonreasons. I did not want anything. It was the least distasteful of the alternatives that occurred to me to fill the hole in a blasted schedule. I don't want to talk about the death of friends, failures of domestic courage, the negative guilt of an ex-patriot. It is probably better to be grieving, tired and guilty in a familiar place. San Francisco is familiar enough, home city as much as I ever had one, growing up American. My great grandparents died there, still speaking German. My mother went to school there, married there with the knees of her bridesmaids showing in both papers. My father went to war with the Japanese from the Oakland Mole. My brother suffered his adolescence in the bars of old North Beach. And I? I used to have lunch with my grandmother in the Palace Hotel, waffles, and the head waiter poured melted

141

butter into each square. She tried to teach me in Chinatown how to recognize Japs by the look of their feet. I had a godmother who sold shoes at the White House because she was divorced. For the same reason my great aunt had a boarding house somewhere out on a street that ran toward the park, where once I spent a whole, terrified night pulling paper off the wall next to my bed. Grandfather had a pass through the restricted areas all during the war. A city of uniforms, of hotel dances and breakfasts at the Cliff House. A familiar place.

Now again it is a city of uniforms, and, learning the newest routines of the airport, I was distressed by them, not resigned as I had been at their age. Most of the boys do not wear their uniforms well, being unfamiliar with ties and used to putting their hands in their trouser pockets. My grandfather would have been critical. I only wondered if they were as clumsy with guns.

A bright, salt smelling day, the first of three. I had no plans. I had written a tentative card to Michael and Jessica, another to Lynn, friends I did not usually see in my funeral and wedding ridden returns. Perhaps I'd see Lawrence. There were half a dozen others. But, of those half dozen, three were on their way to jail. I read that in the *Chronicle* in my slot of a hotel room — The Hilton, which would take more defensive explanation than is valuable. Lawrence was pleading not guilty to disturbing the peace in an anti-draft demonstration. He was trying to disturb the war, he said. Last time I came home my mother said, while we were still at the airport, "You're not going to get involved in any of these marches, are you, darling? You really don't have time to go to jail." It would have been unseemly of me, surely, having given up my citizenship years ago for positive political reasons, for wanting a vote where I lived.

I don't like being ten floors above ground. In San Francisco, every time I am over three floors up, I have fantasies of riding a mattress to Alcatraz, a journey several of us were in the process of attempting when we were discovered and ordered out of the attic. I don't remember whose attic — perhaps my godmother's. Now I understand it is possible to go to Alcatraz by boat, but visiting an empty prison two days before Christmas has no point when old friends are crowded into newer jails.

I had done my Christmas shopping, but I went out into the summer day. The third floor of the City of Paris hasn't been redecorated since my grandmother shopped there. The White House is gone, and my godmother has died of cancer. People are still meeting under the clock at the St. Francis, a dark place, where old men sit and visit on couches just outside the ladies' room. The bar hasn't changed much since my brother and father had one of their many man-to-boy talks twenty years ago, my brother not knowing what to do with a new hat.

I bought books, *Nat Turner* and *All the Little Live Things*, knowing from the reviews that the one would take the last of my irrational liberal hopes that we'd get through without a massacre, that the other would reconfirm the bitter war between the generations, old men drinking themselves to death in Puritan rage, young men hallucinating in tree houses. Is reading a way of not seeing for myself?

Back at the hotel, the red button on my phone was flashing. I had to read a number of directions before I received two messages, one that Michael had appeared "in person", another that Lynn had phoned. And there was a small, live Christmas tree on the desk, about as tall as the bottle of scotch next to it. No card, but it was an unthreatening, discreet kindness. Outside a bus signaled to turn with a high, repeating whistle.

Dinner with Michael and Jessica: the cab driver believed
— because of my foreign clothes and shifting accent? — that
I had confused streets with avenues. He gave ethnic reports
for each more deteriorating neighborhood we passed through.
And finally in the block that should have been Michael's, he
wanted to turn back. But I saw that one of the Victorian
town houses was embarrassed by a nearly completed front
porch. I said to the still very reluctant driver, stopped in the
middle of the street, shining his police flashlight up the
fourteen feet to the front door, that I wanted to get out. He
honked, a thing my father says gentlemen do not do. I
suppose ladies are not expected to have horns to honk. There
was Michael, hurrying down the uncertain new steps, black
hair to his shoulders, his side burns white and winged, the
bones of his face sharp, the flesh soft, his eyes permanently
crossed, caught in their inward gaze by the driver's flashlight.

"This is the place," I said, money ready.

Michael waved the cab away, honking his voice, tenor,
nasal. I saw his velvet shirt, the kind I like to buy for myself
in men's shops. Around his neck, hanging by a black shoe
lace, was a silver lion's head, not medallion so much as door
knocker, Metro Goldwyn Mayer. Michael and I are profes-
sional rather than personal friends. It was a formal moment
before he showed me the path through hardening concrete
up to the unfinished entrance. I had not been to the house
before because it was new to them. Jessica waited just the
other side of the new wrought iron gates, framed in stained
glass. She is tall, cowboy faced, gentle. We were glad to see
each other in this kindness they were offering me.

Other people were there, a couple of close friends in
the habit of the place, which is a stage set, room by high
ceilinged room. We went nearly at once to Michael's studio
on the second floor to see his new paintings, as thick with oil

as relief maps, from photographs and prints of nineteenth century scientific apparatus and bubble gum cards of the Beatles. They would not be properly dry for a hundred years, and then those small mountain ranges of paint would crack into colors of earlier images, flower into the past, or explode. Michael and I would not be there to see it happen, sharing the generation between the great earthquake and his own.

With drinks that Jessica had brought us, we climbed higher. The walls of the old house have little plaster left from years of a leaking roof, but paintings have been hammered to the old lathing, crowded together up the huge stairwell and along the corridors. The windows that are not stained glass are hung with ancient materials, shawls, rugs, tapestries. On the third floor we found the children, a boy and a girl in their early teens, long haired, bare footed, dressed in jeans and sweaters. They were sitting on the floor and did not greet us.

"Med," Michael explained. "Meditation. It keeps them off pot and away from liquor."

We went down by the back stairs, which cut across the wall of the first floor toilet, in use as we passed, and turned into the kitchen, where Jessica was cooking.

"How do you like the house?" she asked.

I did not have to answer because the children, having given us time for our slow descent, came quickly and noisily out of their perch of silence, talking like competing commercials or poems.

"To find out if you had a vision or I had a vision," I said, dated by as well as detached from Ginsberg.

"But it works," North said, friendly now and hopeful.

"If you don't cheat," Sky modified as a way of threatening her brother.

Their odd first names are practical to counteract the

pages of their last name in any telephone directory. And North has the arctic eyes of his father, but straight. Sky is still child enough to be all style without distinctive definition. They are not so much badly brought up children as unbrought up. What manners they use have the charm of their own invention.

Charlie came out of the bathroom, looking for his drink.

"Charlie doesn't even hold it," North said. "The greatest aim in the west."

Jessica was giving us all things to carry into the dining room, where uncertain chairs were randomly placed at a large, round table. Michael and Jessica sat side by side. The rest of us took places we chose or where we found ourselves. Charlie, between the children, took their hands for a moment. It might have been some sort of grace.

"It's a small table now that everyone's in jail," Sky said.

"And you think everybody over eighteen should be in jail," Charlie said. He was obviously over eighteen but not by very many years. "You're a very uncool person, Sky."

"Is it embarrassing to be out of jail?" I asked.

"Yes," Michael said. "It's so easy for me to stay out."

"I'm going when I'm eighteen," North said. "If they get Charlie."

"They're not going to get me," Charlie assured him, "As soon as I get my degree, I'm going to Canada."

"Maybe you won't have to go," Jessica said. "Maybe nobody will."

"Dr. Spock's going to jail," Sky said.

"He's a very uncool man," Charlie answered her.

"What about Lawrence? What about Joan Baez? and her mother? One of my teachers goes to jail every week-end."

"Well, what does one do?" Michael asked. "Even Jessica

146

read Spock when she was scared. He didn't intend to raise a generation of murderers."

"They're building concentration camps for Negroes and draft dodgers," North said. "They're going to evacuate all of Oakland."

"We're going with them," Sky said. "When the time comes."

"Why doesn't somebody teach these kids to be cool? The country's a jail already. You don't have to go anywhere."

I tasted Jessica's bland food, as gentle and vague as her face, and felt the chair under me give slightly. The children were talking now about a college president who was on probation for refusing to let police turn tear gas and dogs against students who were not rioting. Jessica kept saying to each new threat, "Maybe it won't happen. Maybe you won't have to," which was surely how North was conceived, how she married, how she came to live in this whimsical fortress, continually singing hopeful little unrealities to her cross-eyed husband and her children. Nobody ever encouraged her. Nobody ever said, "No, maybe it won't, Jessica. Maybe we won't have to." Nobody believed her because Jessica was basically one of Charlie's uncool people who had been to jail on principle and off principle until Michael found her and kept in mind what could happen and stopped her. If she was less interesting now than she had been in the days of McCarthy purges and the first UN delegation, she was herself safer in a less safe world.

Some time between the main course and dessert, the chair I was sitting on disintegrated. After Charlie and Michael helped me up, the children counted eighteen pieces which they carried in to the fireplace in the living room where another bundle of sticks which had also been a chair waited to be burned.

I keep not mentioning Alice. At first I thought she was with Charlie. Then it seemed to me that she might live in the house. She did not say very much. She kissed one or another of the familiar company now and then, more affectingly when she chose Jessica, who obviously liked to touch her since she was of sweeter, safer substance than the rest of us. Or that would have been my reason for liking to touch her. After dinner she read some poems to us, not clearly her own though she did not disclaim them. They were as diffusely erotic as she was and might have been written for her. The children meditated in various, undisciplined postures, until they fell asleep, in random touch with one or another adult. We were free then to talk of things other than draft dodging, race riots, and drugs. Michael wanted to talk about photographs, those fixed hallucinations from which he worked. Near him was a portrait he had done of old Mrs. Winchester from a photograph, not looking frightened of the things she was frightened of. On his lap was a box of photographs of himself as a child, of machines, of boxers, of Alice, to whom I looked for some explanation. There was none.

At midnight, Charlie drove me back to the Hilton with only a trace of embarrassment, and I invited him to visit me as I always invite people to visit. My phone was flashing with new messages, and there was no direction for stopping it without receiving them.

In the morning, I had Christmas cards with foreign post marks, and out in the bright day a Salvation Army band played by a place advertising topless lunches. In the dining room an Hawaiian tour had just arrived, fifty dyspeptic grandparents with midwestern accents, stricken with pleasures they would rather have read about than paid for. One couple had apparently missed the plane, but they were there somehow, moving from table to table relieving people with their simple anger.

San Francisco is not a beautiful city, except at the distance from it I usually keep. From Berkeley, from Sausalito, from nearly anywhere else, even the sky, it is white and as abruptly mountainous as one of Michael's paintings. But in the city are the centers of pretentious civic architecture, green domes and irrational spires among a cluttered, dwarfed, bay-windowed suburbia. I went to the parks, to the museums, to the cliffs above the Golden Gate, that narrow channel of catastrophes. Across it was a military installation on a golden winter hill with a large, outlined Christmas star for night shining. I went to Cost Plus and bought Korean brass and postcards from Vietnam.

Dinner with Lynn: Christmas Eve is not a time to go out for dinner; so many French, Italian, and Mexican restaurants shut. Lynn came to the hotel, dressed in a carefully tailored suit, stiff collared blouse and cameo where a tie might have been. Soft-haired, soft spoken, amusement and surprise always faint in her face. We had a drink in the hotel while we decided where to go. The exposed thighs of our forty-year-old waitress were not appetizing. Still, we had another drink.

"If we have to choose," Lynn said, "I'd rather have tits."

"Not for dinner. There must be an unbelieving Mexican or Frenchman somewhere in the city."

There was, in Ghirardelli Square. We walked through the shops first, stepping over clay hens and carp, barnacled with succulants, looking at nests of bright boxes, primary colors everywhere. At a shop for child art, a woman was handing out pamphlets for the protection and support of the imagination. The drawings and paintings on display were obviously teacher chosen, either psychiatric or rigid with the right ideas, but occasionally a child had been wilfully childish: a tall house among giant flowers, a sun round in the corner, every object with a face, a bright face. Out in the square itself all the Christmas lights were white, a relief.

We ordered guacamole with a third martini, drank and watched the traffic under and across the bridge. Then we ate the hot food that reminded me of country fairs and my grandmother's cleaning woman, depression food in expensive surroundings. Lynn will not talk unless she is asked questions. I ask questions, thin and general, because I don't know much about efficiency engineering.

"I'm all right now, but there's less and less space to move."

"Why?"

"Nearly everything is war industry."

"And you don't want to work in war industry?"

"Oh, I don't care about that. Simply being alive is murderous. Beyond that, moral choice is a theoretical exercise. The point is I can't work in war industry. I can't get security clearance."

"Why not?"

Lynn smiled with derisive sweetness.

"Is it that bad?"

"When the security people come to ask me about friends I had in graduate school, they ask two questions: is he homosexual and has he ever been to a psychiatrist."

"They wouldn't stop someone who'd been to a psychiatrist," I said.

"I don't know, but there are a lot of people who think it's pretty risky to go to one."

"It's getting very bad," I said.

"I think about getting out, going to Canada, but there's not much for me yet in Canada."

"I suppose not."

"Never mind. I'm having a lovely time. Most people are. A lot of money and a taste of illegality in nearly everything takes care of it."

There is no point ever in arguing with Lynn. Ideas for her are no more than wry confessions. To debate failures of conscience is inappropriate. She paid for my dinner, and we went out to find her car, which I would have been impressed by if I knew anything about cars. I knew only that much. We drove over the hills and out to the Haight-Ashbury district.

"The flower children are almost gone," Lynn said. "There are a couple of good bars."

I was not properly dressed, being properly dressed, in navy silk with a green silk coat. I have other kinds of clothes, even a pair of modest boots, which I would have been glad of, but in whatever costume I would have to carry my age. It becomes me, defining and refining a person out of the blur of adolescence, but persons are troublesome in the places Lynn wanted to go. She's eight years younger than I, the acceptable side of thirty.

As we walked down a quiet side street, we could hear people singing Christmas carols in an apartment above us. One hundred miles to the south, my family had gathered for the same purpose: parents, brother, sisters, nieces and nephew decorating a tree. I had not gone home for Christmas for fifteen years. Only deaths and marriages. My arrival on the twenty-sixth would be without excuse, no relative left to say good-bye to, my parents settled in the static status of the sixties, in my own generation first and even second marriages achieved, the new generation still being measured in steps and inches.

The bar was so crowded that at first we didn't realize we had walked into a Christmas Eve party. Not only all the bar stools and chairs had been taken, but it was difficult to move through the clusters of standing people. A huge man, probably the only man in the place, dressed in a Santa Claus suit, handed us chits for free drinks.

"The bouncer," Lynn explained.

She went to get us drinks, leaving me to occupy what space I could find. I moved farther into the room where a pool table had been covered, obviously ready for food. Only a few people leaned against it; so I joined them without being friendly. On a wall near the juke box was a sign which read, "Pool Table Reserved for Ladies and their Guests." Eight or nine couples were trying to dance, youngsters most of them, some in stylish hip hugging trousers and nearly transparent shirts, others in earnest drag, everything from conservative business suits to motorcycle outfits. They were having fun. It felt like a party, and I was smiling vaguely at it by the time Lynn got back. She had two college students with her, one tall sulky girl in a very well tailored slack suit whose name was Ann, one short dandy with cropped curly hair, a pin-striped suit out of the thirties, and a cigarette holder. She wanted Lynn to dance; so Ann and I held drinks and braced ourselves against the table.

"Tourist?" she asked.

"Not really."

I hadn't been in this kind of bar since my own college days when I was a tourist, but not simply in this world — in all worlds of social definition. Now, careful to have unoffending costumes for most circumstances, I was still, as a traveler, often caught in the wrong one.

"Lynn said you wouldn't want to stay."

"I'm traveling," I said. "I haven't much time."

It was too noisy to talk anyway; so we drank our drinks. then drank the ones we were holding for the other two, and watched the crowd. I was putting my second glass down on the pool table when Ann put an arm around my shoulder. It startled me until I realized why she had done it. A motorcycle rider, nearly as tall as the bouncer, heavy set and handsome, was approaching us.

"Taken?" she said to Ann.

"An old friend from out of town," Ann said carefully.

The explanation was acceptable apparently. The cycle rider nodded and moved on.

"We'd better dance," Ann said.

I hadn't been on a dance floor for perhaps ten years, but only a few of these dancers shook themselves and stared at their own feet. Most of them liked the public declaration of being in each other's arms. I could dance the way I was being asked to. The novelty of it for me, the grace and protectiveness of my partner, were new pleasures. Once I caught sight of Lynn, watching, with that characteristic faintness of surprise and amusement, and I wondered what kind of fool I was making of myself. It was difficult to determine. I am not used to this kind of attention and protection. If dancing had occurred to me, I would have expected to ask.

"Drink?" Ann suggested.

"May I buy it?"

She looked down at me, obviously calculating what that would mean, ready to be agreeable.

"Just to buy it," I said. "I can't stay long."

"Then I'll buy it."

"Like?" Lynn asked, free for a moment from her dandy.

"She's sweet," I said, "but I can't stay around being a hazard."

"What makes you think you're a hazard?"

"These clothes. This age. I haven't any business letting kids take care of me."

"Why not? She wants to. She'd like you to stay."

"How often do you come here?"

"A couple of times a week, I guess."

The questions I hadn't asked at dinner could not be asked now. Still I began to ask.

"Why? What's happened to Jill?"

"She got married last year," Lynn said, "to a very good security risk."

"Still . . ."

"Let's stay another hour, all right?" Lynn interrupted. She had just seen someone she obviously wanted to see. "Then we'll go if you like."

The girl Lynn greeted was with someone else. The tension was unpleasant.

"You don't really like it here, do you?" Ann said, handing me a drink.

"It's a very good party. Thank you."

"We could go some place else."

Lynn was dancing.

"Who is that?" I asked.

"The one with Lynn? I don't know . . . any more. She used to be a friend of mine. Why did you let Lynn bring you here? And why is she embarrassing you like this?"

"She's not," I said. "We're old friends."

"That's all?"

"That's all."

"I didn't know anything was like that any more. Let's dance."

This time it was not easy to do. There was something wrong between Lynn and Ann, a competitiveness.

"We're going down the street for a quiet drink," Ann said to Lynn. "We'll be back in about an hour."

"Why don't I call you at the hotel?" Lynn said, obviously wanting to be helpful.

"All right," I said. Out on the street, I said to Ann, "Let's find a cab for me, and you go back to the party."

But she was hurt; so I walked along with her until we found a bar that was not having a party. I had already had enough to drink, and so had she. I wondered if she was twenty-one.

"I want plain soda," I said.

"Two plain sodas."

"Why are you by yourself on a Christmas Eve?" I asked.

"Why are you?"

"An error in the schedule," I said. "That's all. It happens when you travel a lot."

"I didn't want to go home."

"Well, neither did I, I guess."

"You aren't gay, are you?"

It's an unanswerable question from my point of view, but I am more often than not doubtful about my point of view.

"Yes," I said, regretting it.

"Then why are we sitting here?"

Why? Because I hadn't the sense to know what mood Lynn was really in, what trouble she was in. Because I had on the wrong clothes. I was also wearing the wrong manners, heterosexual, middle-aged manners which involve so many frankly empty gestures.

"We're sitting here because I don't know what else to do."

"I don't understand."

"I know you don't. Shouldn't I take a cab before I begin to give you motherly advice out of sheer embarrassment? I haven't been in that kind of bar since I was your age —

fifteen . . . twenty years ago? It's no time for me to begin. And, as for you, you're not supposed to trust anyone over thirty."

She smiled then, for the first time, and I relaxed a little until she said, "But I think older women are wildly attractive."

"I do, too."

"Oh."

"But not in bars," I went on. "I like them in their own living rooms or on lecture platforms or in offices. I've never danced with one."

"I was only trying to be polite," Ann said.

"I know, and I'm touched by it, but there isn't any way to be polite to me."

"I don't want to go back there either," she said. "Let me stay with you, just for the evening. We could go to a movie or just drive around or go back to my apartment."

Christmas Eve: I should have been in my own apartment cooking a turkey or at home eating one. Or I should have, given all the wrong choices so far, found Lynn and made her take me home to hers, for her own sake, but she did not want to go. Ann and I walked back to the party to make sure. Then we walked again to find Ann's car. I did not want to stay in these remnant crowds, the dying market of flowers. We drove to North Beach and walked in Chinatown. I suppose the shops have always been full of dull, dirty jokes, but I looked for the miniature worlds I loved when I was a child, not stocking presents for the tired and impotent. At midnight, when we might have been in church, we were in my hotel room, drinking scotch, I in the chair by the window, Ann stretched long on one of the beds.

"I'm essentially a very uncool person," she said.

I yawned, thinking of Charlie.

"Merry Christmas," she said.

"Merry Christmas."

I got up to pour a last drink, saw Ann watching me in the mirror, and felt guilty. It did not very much matter to me what I did on this particular evening. At her age, I would have wanted very badly whatever I wanted.

"I feel like a bouncer in Santa Claus disguise," I said.

"You won't have to throw me out. I'll go."

I sat down on the bed beside her. She didn't move. I put a hand on her thigh, and she turned a little toward me, but she did not reach out. I was, for a moment, surprised, then relieved into having to give more than permission. She wanted me as I am used to being wanted by a woman . . . never mind that length of body, the boyish manners. I wanted to laugh, to tease her, but I was afraid to. Her body was so young under my hands, her need so seriously sacred. I was afraid, too, that she would come to me before I had even undressed her or that she would not come at all if I moved too slowly. I had to be very careful, very gentle, control the comic wonder I felt in myself, wanting not simply to be good in bed out of thoughtful habit but to be marvelous at once. But she was as understated and as graceful as she had been on the dance floor, leading only to invite being led, if I had noticed, if I had wanted to notice. She came to me perfectly at the moment I wanted her to.

"You did want me."

"Apparently," I said, and then I did laugh, surprised by her immediate and confident change of mood.

"You wear such pretty clothes."

I am not either twenty or practiced in adjusting my own desire to strangers. The few experiences of this sort that I have had in the last ten years have always embarrassed me and, to some extent, made me feel guilty. I don't believe in fidelity, though it is for me the only practical way to live.

"Don't do that," Ann was saying to me. "Don't go away from me like that."

"I'm sorry."

I must have natural bad manners in bed. I had also had too much to drink. I drifted toward her touch for a moment, enjoying it, then drifted away near sleep.

"I'm sorry," she said.

"How old are you?"

"Eighteen."

"You ought to go home," I said.

Once she had, I couldn't sleep. I read until seven in the morning, ordered breakfast in my room, then took *All the Little Live Things* up to the roof and sat in seventy degrees of sun by an empty swimming pool until a woman joined me who wanted to know if I thought the deck chairs at the Athens Hilton weren't better than these.

"I haven't been to the Athens Hilton."

"The chairs are better. I have trouble with my back."

I turned a page.

"They ought to be all the same. It's a chain, after all."

I closed my book and took the elevator to the lobby. There was a telegram. I sent a reply and then walked up the street to *David's* for lunch, lox and cream cheese. When I paid the bill, the cashier handed me a small box. Out on the street, I opened it to find four large macaroons and the message, "Eat thy macaroons with joy. David."

I went back and bought two dozen macaroons. Then I went to my room, closed my suitcases and phoned my brother. He would meet the bus.

And say "How's the picture business, Sis?" or "Mother's worried there aren't enough sweet potatoes," or "It's like you to be the only goy at David's on Christmas day." It's a long ride on the Bayshore which has tabled out over the years so that there are no landmarks left, forests or hills of flowers, nothing except occasional hangers, faint structures in the haze.

What he did say was, "I think I'm going to Vietnam next week."

Christmas dinner at home:

"They give them estrogen, that's all. When they're about eight or nine. They stop growing and start developing. And if it's a matter of having to wear a bra in the fifth grade or go through life six feet tall . . ."

"Harry sent off to Charles Atlas and got this questionnaire about whether or not he was popular. 'Are you constipated?' 'Do you have bad breath . . .'"

"Charles Atlas must be one hundred and two."

"Aren't you proud of your brother going off to Vietnam? They'll only send him where it's safe, of course, just where the President goes."

"Friends of ours won't even take a plane that flies *over* France."

"It's easier to share a crust of bread than a feast, that's why. I mean, if all you have is a crust of bread, who cares?"

"I showed the cops where I found it — a whole great big sack of it, just sitting in a tree. I was looking for snakes."

"People with long hair want to go to jail."

"She said all the men who go to concerts are queer. I said, 'Well, George isn't.' She's just jealous."

"Every year I think I like the pink camelia best until the white one comes out, and then I just can't make up my mind."

"Why decide?"

"I like to know what I like."

159

"If you want to know what I think, I think Charles Atlas is dead."

"Then who's reading his mail? That's illegal."

"Look, a bra in the fifth grade is an asset. Ask Harry."

"I think saying grace in Latin is phoney. God speaks English, doesn't He?"

"We learned *Jingle Bells* in Latin."

"It's going to be a long war, that's all."

"Is the turkey dry?"

"Not the dark meat. I suppose you're used to goose."

"Poets live in trees."

"Don't argue about it; discuss it."

They all have names, and I have no trouble remembering them. In fact, I say their names too often when I'm talking to them. I have loved the children, each one. But Harry, the oldest, my brother's son, is most familiar to and with me. He invited me to see the workout room he was digging out under the garage. And, while I stood, admiring the hole in the ground, he took off his jacket, tie and shirt, and reached for his pick axe. I watched the easy rhythm of his young muscles, the sun on his California color hair. He hadn't been at work for more than five minutes when I looked up to see a girl sitting on the stone fence, then another in the apple tree. They perched as still as birds.

"How old are you, Harry?"

"Nearly old enough," he said seriously.

Mother was calling from across the yard. "It's long distance, dear."

I never have any trouble deciding for the white camelia.

"That isn't what 'homesick' means exactly," I said into the phone. "Yes, sell it." And then to the question of how long I would be away, "Long enough to say good-bye to Harry."

It shouldn't have come as a surprise.

"Oh, screw the kids," my brother was saying. "It's Christmas and I want another drink."

Charles Atlas isn't dead; it's the children who are mortal. Now that grandparents are all dead, now that everyone who is going to marry has married, it is time to say good-bye to the children. I came home to say good-bye to North and Sky and Ann and Harry.

Invention
for Shelagh

"What does your face mean now?"

"I'll write it to you," I say, and Shelagh smiles, easy, knowing either I really will or that I'll tell her some other time when there aren't quite so many people as there are now: Haron, Leith, Fran, as well as Shelagh, Helen and I. Or maybe, in a way, Shelagh's reading my face and letting me know, the way she lets Haron know by touching him.

When I get home, I go to my desk, open my journal and write: Shelagh's space-place (in me?)

The post American gothic window, Leith's American gothic face. That's what broke it open for me — immediate nourishment? — what came then was how much in that space I'd cast there, not just Grandmother's maroon plates and cups, her card table, Helen's mother's chairs, but *even* Haron. How much challenged me there — the Bridget Riley poster — never mind Doris Lessing. The old records, which do make me remember Garberville as well as private South Fork. And how does it happen a) that Shelagh doesn't really want me there for a year and b) that I find my imagination, scattered for months in interesting but thin places, coming together in the fragments of her place. One image: that I'm a piece of pottery smashed, the shards everywhere. Another: in Shelagh's space I am finally the altogetherness of being about to make a coherent statement. And I *really* wonder what it's like for her to live in *our* space. Does that complex focus of herself happen to her? I wrote an edgy story out of her cottage on the lane. If this isn't simply drunken sharp edges, I'd like to write "Shelagh's space-place" from zoo sheets to rock-plexiglass rock-actual room, a love song of how we put each other together in nephews and plates and loving Helen. And this vision is partly an assertion against my grief about Doris Lessing, the immediacy of not wanting Fran to ride on that bird, Helen to distance herself so much as not to be primarily offended, Shelagh to be wooed by *any* energy. I do feel as if I knew, with passion, about the wrong of that book, as simple as knowing the lobster is bad, don't eat it. And have the vocabulary, but not shared, to say so: to say Don't. For the sake of Life, DON'T. And feel guilt only because of the urgency I have to make my own vision clear. my love: Haron and Leith and Shelagh and Fran and Helen, I love you. Don't ride on that bird. It's a chairlift into arrogant desolation, into a lie about not only the stars but ourselves. I, who live daily close to madness and its wily justifications, love too much to go there, and I cannot stand anyone else taking an energy ride out of that perverse imagination. But I don't want my power to cut out. I wanted to go away, to live in myself, unoffending, somewhere else.

Notes for me, not for Shelagh.

"I'll write it to you" doesn't weigh on my conscience, but it does on my imagination. Shelagh and I talk about writing sometimes, writing to each other, and we sometimes have, but not ever, or not yet, in the way we imagine we might. Our letters have been personal. Personal doesn't mean anything. Timely, then, about planes to meet, changes of plan, ongoing fragments of our own and our friends' lives. What we have in mind instead is some kind of elaborate conversation, I think, and I could try to write, from those notes, a letter. Or I could simply read those notes to Shelagh and we could talk. But I want to climb up through process to make something, as I understand it and can come to understand it. And that is what I meant when I said, "I'll write it to you."

The way the maze at Hampton Court this summer is something other than how Shelagh wrote about it to Haron or how we all learn to tell it together at parties now that we are out of it and at home. My maze? My invention? Well, yes. And I'll wait to know what that is, as I waited for months before we went into the maze with the tag line, "Something amazing, a boy falling out of the sky." And never once thought of myself as Icarus, never mind Daedalus, some sort of old testament woman rather, with a face like dissolving rock under the heat of someone else's mortal fire. And still do, obviously, as I shout at Fran. "Get off Doris Lessing's bird!" And get out of that two bit satire about the Greek gods. You, too, I want to say to myself, feeling a brief temptation of my own.

Shelagh writes on her walls on strips of newsprint. The people who visit often, like Leith and Haron, have to choose whether to read what is written there or not. Shelagh reads what she has written to Helen and me after she has taken it down, typed it and carried it 7000 miles. Shelagh takes down her walls and brings them to England. We sit in our rented house there and listen to her walls. That is how Shelagh makes home with us. Her nephews come and build roads and airstrips in the rock garden. Helen and Shelagh and I can cook together in a space four feet square. We think of putting flour on the floor to see how our feet do it. Shelagh is the only one who always remembers to give the gardener his tea. Shelagh got us out of the maze that day. "The way out is the way in," she said. We followed her there. Out. Without flour or bread crumbs. Otherwise Helen would have slashed down the privet hedge with the power of her imagination. One of us always does something.

We showed Shelagh the house in Chelsea where we might have stayed. She and Helen both believed that somehow they could have imagined themselves into it, though neither would have wanted to. We went through it like tourists, and I could see the invisible velvet ropes strung across bedroom doors, but Shelagh and Helen went in, set feet right down on the carpets, pointed at the drapes, found the cracks in the wall paper that were cupboard doors, peered at a white china blue bird in a niche, and said to each other, "We could have done it. We could." I couldn't. It was hard enough to crack an ice tray open and pour drinks from my own bottle in that parody of a rich man's town house, all mirrors and crystal chandeliers. In the maid's room there is a picture of a cow mooing. But in that room also there are bars on the windows. *I* got us out of there.

Written in my journal at 1:40 a.m.: "Rereading what I wrote today — 'Invention for Shelagh' it's probably called — I have a fantasy about phoning her now, saying, 'this is suicide time' — like that kid at Concord who couldn't ask to talk after lights were out unless she'd done something as important as slitting her wrists. Sexual tides, Shelagh's and mine, sometimes pull us apart. I wonder if she knows my regret as well as I sometimes know hers, not for lack of sexual saying between us, for the tides themselves. We are generous there, too. Shelagh never takes suicide space. Neither do I. I give us stars for that. Should I?"

In the light of day, yes. Suicide space excludes the whole clutter of living which we so welcome in each other. Shelagh says, "I've decided there should be one slob in the house, and I'm it." Because she likes books and clothes and old coffee cups to decide for themselves, a democracy of objects about her. I bully what I own, order furniture and china and papers about in military frenzy. Helen coaxes things into place, makes them comfortable where they belong. Is it because there is no morality in it that Shelagh can late at night set the breakfast table with me as companionably as if we were laying out a game of double solitaire? She has done it even on her way home to her own place, simply to set me in order where I like to be. But playing our orderly games in her own place is too much more than once a year, borrowing chairs from Larry so that everyone can sit at the table, gathering up all the papers, making the bed so that Haron can show off the fine zoo sheets he's brought back from California. They wake to leering giraffes and smug hippopotomuses. Haron's jeans hang in careful arrangement against one living room wall, the ones he drew on the first time he dropped acid, complementing Bridget Riley. The serial photographs of rocks are mounted as if in an art gallery, VERY IMPORTANT, the rock itself on the floor on a piece of paper. The writing walls are in the bedroom. Shelagh, when she orders things, does so to see them. My order makes things invisible, as if I were preparing for black-out or blindness and only cared not to stumble. Looking, really looking, at anything but the human face is something I have to remind myself to do. Without Helen, without Shelagh I would go functionally blind for days at a time.

I stay home, go out, travel, to see people. I simply learn

to complain at the Tate about the heads that get in the way of the paintings. Only a remarkable portrait is more interesting than any face in the crowd, no portrait as interesting as Helen's face or Shelagh's face looking at it. The Turners? They force me to acknowledge the existence of the sky. Take away the human face. Take away the sky under which I occasionally know I live. Offer me in geometric metaphor the quality of light, the tension of objects in space, the absolute command of the vision to be seen, my eyes torn free of their migraine, myopic defenses, I will resist. Helen and Shelagh walk me through the Hayward Gallery to see the Bridget Riley show as if I were just out of hospital. The guards all wear sun glasses, characters in a Cocteau movie. The spaces of the rooms are as huge and empty as the space in dreams, nothing there to order into invisibility, only the commands on the walls. Know with your eyes. Helen has such natural courage, Shelagh such joy in the energy, the acute intelligence. I couldn't go alone into that light, and, even now, two months later, Shelagh and Helen appear to me as much nurses and jailors as companions in that space.

If the escape from the peopled maze is into a Bridget Riley painting, then I *am* Icarus falling into the sea.

We all three need so much more of the world than any one is willing to risk alone that each of us can agree, for a time, to be invalid victim to another's courage. Is that true? It is for me. Helen would have other words for it; so would Shelagh, who asked once this summer after serving one of my invented days, "Is it worth it. . . for you?" "Yes," I said. And grew a little moral vision from that exchange but don't know that will transplant to any other occasion.

When Shelagh defended me against Rick's charge that I was 'good with people', she wanted nothing of the con artist in it, nothing of manipulation. I did what I cared to do, caring about people. Yes. But I have taught us all automatic pilot amiability so that we can not only cook in four square feet but stand to linear hours of people without knowing how we do it. I rarely ask why either. But I do know, yes. If I am on those occasions sometimes nurse and jailor as well as companion, I can be.

On a train from Wallington to London, a sick child howls, monotonous, as rhythmic as breathing, either retarded or very ill, perhaps both. Everyone in the carriage is restless. Someone shouts 'Shut up!" We wait through a long four minutes to the next station, get out and get into another carriage, not sharing whatever guilty or fearful memories we might have, sharing only the resolution to move. We usually sit through even bad plays, as helpless to change them, perhaps as troubled, but we talk afterwards about Osborne's stinking, stupid politics, the 'acky-acky-acky' melodrama of the last act, and finally laugh about the exact duplication of Haron's holey jeans on the stage American who is allowed only, "Shit, shit, shit" to articulate the revolution. About the child we say nothing.

Shelagh says the pictures Helen took this summer are full of processions of asses. I had noticed instead how often we walked or stood, apparently inattentive to each other, like horses in a field; beyond the backs of our heads, the characteristic body stances, always a great tower or an expanse of field. The pictures Avis took in the house, the pictures Helen has taken over the years at home, show us either alone for the camera, Helen picking flowers, Shelagh modeling her new trousers, me writing my journal, or obviously together at the breakfast or dinner table, engaged. I don't feel sorry for us in those large landscapes, but there is something about us that is always a bit bewildered, patient, abstracted under Turner skies.

The pictures my mind took: Shelagh at Victoria station, Gate 9, with pack sack, straw basket, brief case, laughing, pleased with herself. "I even have my ticket." (My snapshots move and talk). Shelagh at the front door, welcoming us home from a week-end, tired of running the house herself but determined to go on with it for the rest of the day. Shelagh and Helen high up behind me on the theater stairs, laughing to each other, with the same relief I feel that we've all made it again. Shelagh and Helen in the upstairs hall late at night, conspiratorial as children who have been told to go straight to bed.

Since Shelagh had posters made for us, I have wanted all memory to be life size. Instead of Che and Mao, Shelagh gave us herself and Ted bottling wine, drunk and hilarious, Helen's mother standing in blue jeans in her beloved farm fields, my grandmother standing in the hollow of a redwood tree. Since, we have added Rick on the Cutty Sark, my great grandmother in a row boat with a good sized steelhead. They are in the garage, along with our Bridget Riley poster, and they are fading with the weather. But I renew rather than replace memory.

"Once you take it all away, getting married, having children, even remembering to comb your hair, what is there left to being female? And does it matter?" Shelagh is sitting next to me in the seminar we share for the Women's Studies' Course and posing the question to fifteen other people but as importantly to herself. Is she tempted to answer it? To try, probably. I'm not sure it is a question for me. But I would go back as far as I had to to remember when it still was. For Shelagh, I would. Years back, then, to about the age of 25 or 26, still vulnerable to descriptions of other women, "She never married", still threatened by the sexual gossip of men looking for 'good tits', 'a piece of ass', and simply frightened by the prospect of taking my life in my own hands, never having taken earning a living very seriously. Could I live with all those tags of failure, no husband, no child, at the bottom of the academic ladder with no inclination to take even the first step up into a PhD, six or seven years of unpublished manuscripts stuffed into filing drawers? "Does it matter?" For the proud and frightened, of course it matters, at that point. And no decision against retreating into the success of MRS or PhD or both is made without pig-headed refusal to be humiliated. The only consolation I had was that no man as proud as I could ever risk it. So what was left? That sense of immunity that is also part of the package of being female. If the world doesn't take you seriously to begin with, your failure in it can't be all that much of a disaster. Yeats' poem about failure, "Be secret and exult." By now I think I have also forgotten or left behind my immunity. As Shelagh leaves hers when she says about getting up to speak before a crowd, "It does matter. If you are going to get up and do it, you've got to leave all that tentativeness and apology behind. It's private. Get through it at home. That's what a bathroom's for. Then stand up and say what you have to say without anything left of being 'just a woman'."

That's one line for the answer to take, and it gets us somewhere but not as far as Shelagh's question pushes. For standing there without any of those conventional definitions, protections, limitations, something is surely left, and it may matter. To ourselves as well as the audience. I really don't know.

For over a year, and more obviously this summer in London, I have been taken as often for a man as for a woman. Shelagh could believe the funny story about the young salesman at my front door, asking first for my mother, then for my wife, finally for 'the lady of the house'. But she did not believe that as often as not during a day, I was called 'sir' rather than 'madame' until we were all getting out of a cab at the theatre. The doorman greeted Helen with "good evening, madam, ." Shelagh with "good evening, miss, ." and me with "good evening, sir." I have not chosen a disguise. I have not changed my hair style or my way of dressing for twenty years. It is men who have grown their hair, put bright scarves around their necks, and altered their voices to gentleness. Their choices have not only changed my social sexual identity but also my age. For lack of a beard, for a low pitched but light voice, I am not a forty year old woman, but a twenty year old boy. There are obviously a number of twenty year old boys, without my height, who are being called 'miss' and still don't find it threatening or humiliating enough to cut their hair.

Last spring, when Gladys had her baby, Shelagh told me she could not bring herself to ask whether it was a boy or a girl. What do we mean by the phrase 'private parts'? What is public sexuality?

A dream reported in my class last night: a young woman was on an operating table, a nurse pushing down on her belly, asking whether she wanted to know now if it was dead or alive. No, she would wait until it was born to be told. The nurse shone a flashlight into her, then ran to get the doctor, a great bulbous man. The young woman then found herself being ushered into a room without furniture. She was exhausted, too uncomfortable to be willing to sit on the floor, very angry. Another young woman in a hospital gown came in and said, "I had a boy. What did you have?" "A light bulb."

The man who delivered a light bulb into the world was proud of it. Why not turn nightmare into day dream or even fact?

172

Stand up with a wedding ring, be eight and a half months pregnant, and you are still 'just a woman'. Add a career. You are not then more but suspected of being even less. So the terms of reference we have won't work. We do have to throw them out, all of them. Yes, the baby with the bath water, the lot. With no immunity, with no certainty at all about what is left, begin again.

Shelagh told me last night that she must go into the hospital in a few days' time to have a cone biopsy. She is under thirty. She has to convince the doctor that the potential of her uterus is not more important to her than the protection of her own life, that his decisions must be based on her set of values rather than his own.

She also said, "It doesn't bother *me* when Helen cries."

In any evening, we all have marvellous ideas, but Shelagh's have a vehemence that Helen remembers, believes, and often acts on the next morning: trying to order a game pie from Selfridge's ("Madame, game is out of season"), dialing a poem. Today I found myself caught up in one of Shelagh's late night schemes, left to me because she has gone out of town for the week-end. I know only half way into it that it is another game pie. So I tell the story out of season.

Are we inclined to see the difficulties in each other's lives and admire the courage rather than the ease which makes our several choices possible? Perhaps I don't think about Shelagh's life when it is easy to. I think of it, apart from mine, only when she is impatiently casting off domestic involvement while at the same time guiltily describing the 'uncomfortable space' she must live in, crowded with people who require and delight her attention.

"I have no domestic peace, except with the two of you here," and she mistrusts herself if she stays in it for very long.

She needs the stress of crowded singularity. There it is, in negative terms. Freedom from domestic involvement, from accountability in those daily terms gives her the energy to spend herself as she does.

Events of any day smash against this invention like birds against my study window. They don't break the glass, but I can't entirely rid the process of that mortal thumping. From Helen's study, she can hear, day after day, the obscene saws and the breaking rush and shudder of the trees going down in the ravine. I don't know Shelagh's sounds. I do know she looks out of her window at a corrugated iron building on which are printed the letters, V.I.E.W.

Helen talks of turning this house into a commune, by which she means that perhaps Shelagh would share it with us. Commune is a word like fuck: political. Not for Helen, for me. I have to walk round it and come in at the private entrance. I am exclusive, hording of my little authorities, jealous of my own time. The smallest shift in responsibility, whether more or less, requires great deliberation. I am more comfortable sharing negative fantasies: room and board somewhere for $85.00 a month. Is having my own money different from simply having money? my own space different from space? Well, I like to give them both away, grandly, and that's ridiculous, so beautifully ridiculous that I might talk myself into one final grand gesture, about which we could all rollick with laughter. I mean, if I put all my vast sums of money into the common till, what's less grand about that than buying Helen a painting or keeping the liquor bill a secret from Shelagh, who knows how much it is anyway? Nobody needs to give up paintings or liquor. And surely I really am past needing to make money for the sake of having made it, to pay for the right to my own space. I don't really need 'my own' in that sense. This house is always a clutter of people, some delighted in, some endured.

While Shelagh moves through restless days toward Thursday's operation, Helen and I are planning menus for Shelagh's mother and then for Shelagh when she comes home. But we are also, in our imaginations, moving beds around and bank accounts. It may be a game pie, but when we dialed a poem, we heard a poem every night for the nights after Shelagh had left England.

Last night Shelagh said, "Maybe we've got rid of the baby, but what about all this bath water?" We were talking with our seminar group about the competition and justification that goes on in relationship. People must ask each other for money and freedom, justify those needs each time they occur. Answers? Pool all moneys, pay for the necessities and divide what is left equally. Assert freedom. Don't ever ask for it. Simple as that. There is resigned laughter from most people in the room, vehement hope only from the young woman who lives in a commune, but she also talks a great deal about limiting one's needs, self-sacrifice, attitudes I don't have much real respect for. Why? She would teach the painter to need no more physical space than the writer, no more money for materials, and sees all such activities essentially as 'hobbies'. I am not interested in anyone's adjusting needs for the sake of a group, for the sake of any other person, except in circumstances of emergency. Shelagh says she does adjust to someone else's need, ignoring her own, until she is furious, which doesn't take long.

"Why should *I* go home when he's sleepy?" she demands. "He can go home any time he likes."

Well, Haron agrees.

Then Shelagh demands, "Why aren't you angry with me?"

A happy fight with ranges of comic anger. We should indulge more in expressing our interior logics, their fierce, ludicrous power. Why translate into the justifiable? I live more comfortably with outrageous needs than moral imperatives, in me and in the people around me.

Leith and both Ricks have called, wanting news of Shelagh. Her mother and Helen and I talk briefly about problems that may come up about visitors while Shelagh is in the hospital. There are so many people.

Haron and Shelagh's mother are sitting in the dining room over morning coffee where last night at nine-thirty she and Ted sat having a late supper. Mrs. Jelking has made another pot of coffee and is now washing windows. Haron has brought Shelagh's clothes and the zoo sheets to wash in our machine. I have just finished reading Reich's *The Sexual Revolution*, an analysis of the failure of communes in Russia.

"When are you going to see Shelagh?" Haron asks me.

"I don't want to be selfish," Shelagh's mother says to me.

I'm not going to the hospital at all unless, for some reason, Shelagh needs to see me. I stay in the center of the house, like someone keeping a boat balanced. That is where I like to be, in my psychic space. There are plenty of people just now to take care of Shelagh. Helen and I take care for her.

"What does your face mean now?"

That I am discovering the space we live in, how incredibly crowded it is with who I am, who each of us is, how much room there seems to be. I don't feel sure footed, but I feel together we are. When I want to know why, I try to read answers in Grandmother's plates, Haron's face, the

Bridget Riley poster, which is as hard and fine as we know how to make Christmas. Or I listen again to what we say to each other. We so rarely get in each other's way. Or maybe like to be there. We do not make laws so much as come upon patterns, those comic, invisible footprints on the kitchen floor, these words on the page.

In the Attic of the House

Alice hadn't joined women's liberation; she had only rented it the main floor of her house. It might turn out to be the alternative to burning it down, which she had threatened to do sober and had nearly accomplished when she was drunk. Since none of the four young women who moved in either drank or smoked, they might be able to save Alice from inadvertence. That was all. And the money helped. Alice had not imagined she would ever be sixty-five to have to worry about it. Now the years left were the fingers of one hand. She was going to turn out to be one of the ones too mean to die.

"I'm a lifer," she said at the beer parlor and laughed until her lungs came to a boil.

"Don't sound like it, Al. If the weed don't get you, the traffic will."

"Naw," Alice said. "Only danger on the road is the amateur drunks, who can't drive when they're sober either. I always get home."

The rules were simple: stay in your own lane, and don't honk your horn. Alice was so small she peered through rather than over her steering wheel and might more easily have been arrested as a runaway kid than a drunk. But she'd never caught hell from anyone but Harriet, rest her goddamned soul. Until these females moved in.

"Come have a cup of tea," one of them would say just as Alice was making a sedate attempt at the stairs.

There she'd have to sit in what had been her own kitchen for thirty years, a guest drinking Red Zinger or some other Koolade-colored wash they called tea, squinting at them through the steam: Bett, the giant postie; Trudy and Jill, who worked at the women's garage without a grease mark under their fingernails; Angel, who was unemployed; young, all of them, incredibly young, killing her with kindness. Sober, she could refuse them with, "I never learned to eat a whole beet with chopsticks," or "Brown rice sticks to my dentures," but once she was drunk and dignified, she was caught having to prove that point and failing as she'd always failed, except that now there was the new test of the stairs.

"Do you mind having to live in the attic of your own house?" Bett asked as she offered Alice a steadying hand.

"Mind? Living on top of it is a lot better than living in the middle of it ever was. I don't think I was meant for the ground floor," Alice confessed, her spinning head pressed against Bett's enormous bosom until they reached the top stair.

"You all right now? Can you manage?"

"Sleep like a baby. Always have."

Alice began to have infantile dreams about those breasts, though awake and sober she found them comically alarming rather than erotic, eye-level as she was with them. Alice liked Bett and was glad, though she didn't hold with women taking over everything, that Bett delivered the mail. Bett had not only yellow hair but yellow eyebrows, a sunny sort of face for carrying the burden of bills as well as the promise of love letters and surprise legacies. And everyone was able to see at a glance that this postie was a woman.

Angel was probably Bett's girl, though Alice couldn't tell for sure. Sometimes Alice imagined four-way orgies going on downstairs, but it could as easily be a karate lesson. It was obvious that none of them was interested in men.

"We don't hate men because we don't need them," said Trudy, the one who memorized slogans; who, once she could fix a car, couldn't imagine what other use men were ever put to.

Hating men, for this crew, would be like hating astronauts, too remote an exercise to be meaningful. Alice knew lots of men, was more comfortable with them than with women at the beer parlor or in the employees' lounge at Safeway, where she worked. As a group, she needed them far more than she needed women. Working among them and drinking among them had always been her self-esteem.

"Aren't you ashamed to sit home on a Saturday night?" Alice asked.

"We don't drink; the bars aren't our scene."

Alice certainly couldn't imagine them at her beer parlor, looking young enough to be jail bait and dressed so badly men who had taken the time to shave and change into good clothes couldn't help taking offense. Even Alice, with her close-cropped hair, put on a nice blouse over good slacks, even sometimes a skirt, and she didn't forget her lipstick.

"Do you buy all your clothes at the Sally Ann?" Alice asked, studying one remarkably holey and faded tank top Jill was wearing.

"Somebody gave me this one," Jill admitted irritably. "Why should you mind? You're the only one of any sex who has a haircut like that."

181

"Don't you like it?" Alice asked.

"It's sort of male chauvinist," Trudy put in, "as if you wanted to come on very heavy."

"I don't come on," Alice said. "I broke the switch."

At the beer parlor someone might have said, "Then I'll screw you in," or something else amiable, but this Trudy was full of sudden sympathy and instruction about coming to terms with your own body, as if she were about to invent sex, not for Alice, just for instance.

"Do you know how old I am?"

"We're not ageists here," Jill said.

"I'm old enough to be your grandmother."

"Not if you're still working at Safeway, you're not. My grandma's got the old-age pension."

"When I was young, we had some respect for old people."

"Everybody should respect everybody," Angel said.

"I have every respect for you," Alice said with dignity. "Even about sex."

"You know what you should do, Alice?" Angel asked. "It's not too late . . . is come out."

"Come out?" Alice demanded. "Of where? This is my house after all. You're just renting the main floor. Come out? To whom? Everyone I know is dead!"

Harriet, rest her goddamned soul. Alice mostly pretended that she never spoke Harriet's name. In fact, she almost always waited to do it until she had drunk that amount which would let her forget what she had said so that she could say it over and over again. "Killed herself in my bathtub. Is that any way to win an argument? Is it?"

"What argument?" Trudy would ask.

"This bathtub?" Jill tried to confirm.

"How?" Angel wanted to know.

Later, on her unsteady way upstairs, Alice would resent most Bett's asking, "Were you in love with Harriet?"

"In love?" Alice demanded. "Christ! I lived with her for thirty years."

Never in those thirty years had Alice ever spoken as openly to Harriet as she was expected to speak with these females. Never in the last twenty years had Alice and Harriet so much as touched, though they slept in the same bed. At first Alice had come home drunk and pleading. Then she came home drunk and mean, sometimes threatening rape, sometimes in a jeering moral rage.

"What have you got to be guilty about? You never so much as soil your hand. I'm the one that should be crawling off to church, for Christ's sake!"

Sometimes that kind of abuse would weaken Harriet's resolve and she would submit, whimpering like a child anticipating a beating, weeping like a lost soul when it was over.

Finally Alice simply came home drunk and slept in a drunken stupor. She learned from the beer parlor how many men did the same thing.

"Scruples," one man explained. "They've got scruples."

"Scruples, shit! On Friday night I go home with the dollars and say, 'You want this? You put out for it.'"

"So what are you doing down here? It's Friday, isn't it?"

"Yeh, well, we split . . ."

Harriet had her own money. She was a legal secretary. Alice remembered the first time she ever saw Harriet in the beer parlor wearing a prim gray suit, looking obviously out of place. Some cousin had brought her and left her for unrelated pleasures. After they'd talked a while, Alice suggested a walk along the beach. It was summer; there was still light in the sky.

Years later, Harriet would say, "You took advantage. I'd been jilted."

Sometimes, when Alice was very drunk, she could remember how appealing the young Harriet had been, how willingly she had been coaxed from kisses to petting of her shapely little breasts, protesting with no more than, "You're as bad as a boy, Al, you really are." "Do you like it?" "Well, I'm not supposed to say so, am I?" Alice also remembered the indrawn breath of surprise when she first laid her finger on that wet pulse, the moment of wonder and triumph before the first crying, "Oh, it must be terrible what we're doing! We're going to burn in hell!"

Harriet could frighten Alice then with her guilt and terror. Once Alice promised that they'd never again, as Harriet called it, "go all the way," if they could still kiss, touch. Guiltily, oh so guiltily, weeks later, when Alice thought Harriet had gone to sleep, very gently she pressed open Harriet's thighs and touched that forbidden center. Harriet sighed in sleeping pleasure. Three or four times a week for several years Alice waited for the breathing signal that meant Harriet was no longer officially aware of what was happening. Alice could mount her, suck at her breasts, stroke and enter her, bring her to wet coming, and hold her until she breathed in natural sleeping. Then Alice would go to the bathroom and masturbate to the simple fantasy of Harriet making love to her.

It wasn't Harriet who finally quit on it. It was Alice, shaking her and shouting, "You goddamned hypocrite! You think as long as you take pleasure and never give it, you'll escape. But you won't. You'll be in hell long before I will, you goddamned *woman!*"

"We're looking for role models," Angel said. "Anybody who lived with anybody for thirty years . . ."

"I don't know what you're talking about," Alice said soberly on her way to work, but late that night she was willing enough. "Thirty years is longer than reality, you know that? A lifetime guarantee on a watch is only twenty. Nothing should last longer than that. Harriet should have killed herself ten years earlier, rest her goddamned soul. I always told her she'd get to hell long before I did."

"What was Harriet like?" Bett asked on the way upstairs.

"Like? I don't know. I thought she was pretty. She never thought so."

"It must be lonely for you now."

"I've never had so much company in all my damned life."

To be alone in the attic was a luxury Alice could hardly believe. It had been her resigned expectation that Harriet, whose soul had obviously not been at rest, would move up the stairs with her. She had not. If she haunted the tenants as she had haunted Alice, they didn't say so. The first time Trudy and Jill took a bath together probably exorcised the ghost from that room, and Harriet obviously wouldn't have any more taste for the vegetarian fare in the dining room than Alice did. As for what probably went on in the various beds, one night of that could finally have sent Harriet to hell where she belonged.

Alice understood, as she never had before, why suicide was an unforgivable sin. Harriet was simply out of the range of forgiveness, as she hadn't been for all her other sins from hoarding garbage to having what she called a platonic relationship with that little tart of a switchboard operator in her office.

"If you knew anything about Plato . . ." Alice had bellowed, knowing only that.

Killing herself was the ultimate conversation stopper, the final saying, "No backs."

"The trouble with ghosts," Alice confided to Bett, "is that they're only good for replays. You can't break any new ground."

Bett leaned down and kissed Alice good night.

"Better watch out for me," Alice said, but only after Bett had gone downstairs. "I'm a holy terror."

That night Harriet came to her in a dream, not blood-filled as all the others had been but full of light. "I can still forgive you," she said.

"For what?" Alice cried, waking. "What did I ever do but love you, tell me that!"

That was the kind of talk she heard at the beer parlor from her male companions, all of whom had wives and girl friends who spent their time inventing sins and then forgiving them.

"My wife is so good at forgiving, she's even forgiven me for not being the Shah of Iran, how do you like that?"

"I like it. It has dignity. My old lady forgives my beard for growing in the middle of the night."

They had also all lived for years with threats of suicide.

"She's going to kill herself if I don't eat her apricot sponge, if I don't cut the lawn, if I don't kiss her mother's ass. I tell her it's okay with me as long as she figures out a cheap way of doing it."

Alice was never drunk enough or off her guard enough until she got home to say, "Harriet did. She killed herself in my bathtub." Nobody at the beer parlor or at work knew that Harriet was dead.

"I didn't ever tell them she was alive," she said to Bett. "So what's the point of saying she's dead?"

"Why do you drink with those people?" Bett asked. "They can't be your real friends."

"How can you say a thing like that?"

"They don't know who you are."

"Do you?" Alice demanded. "What has a woman bleeding to death in my bathtub got to do with who I am?"

Bett was pressing Alice's drunken head against her breast.

That night Alice fell asleep with a cigarette in her hand. When she woke, the rug was on fire. She let out a bellow of terror and began to try to stamp out the flames with her bare feet.

Jill was the first one to reach her, half drag, half carry her out of the room. Trudy and Bett went in with buckets of water while Angel phoned the fire department.

"Don't let the firemen in," Alice moaned, sitting on Harriet's old chair in their old living room. "They'll wreck the place."

The fire was out by the time the truck arrived. After the men had checked the room and praised presence of mind and quick action for saving the house, the fire chief said, "Just the same, one of these nights she's going to do it. This is the third time we know of."

Jill, with the intention of confronting Alice with that fact, was distracted with discovering that Alice's feet were badly burned.

The pain killers gave Alice hallucinations: the floor of her hospital room on fire, her nurse's hair on fire, the tent of blankets at the foot of her bed burning, and Harriet was shouting at her, "We're going to burn in hell."

"Please," Alice begged. "I'd rather have the pain."

In pain, she made too much noise, swore, demanded whiskey, threatened to set herself on fire again and be done with it, until she was held down and given another shot.

Her coworkers from Safeway sent her flowers, but no one she worked with came to see her. No one she drank with knew what had happened. From the house, only Bett came at the end of work, still dressed in her uniform.

"Get me out of here," Alice begged. "Can't you get me out of here?"

In the night, with fire crackling all around her, Alice knew she was in hell, and there was no escape, Bett with her sunny face and great breasts the cruelest hallucination of all.

Even on the day when Bett came to take her home, Alice was half-convinced Bett was only a devilish trick to deliver her to greater torment, but Alice also knew she was still half-crazy with drugs or pain. There the house still stood, and Bett carried her up the stairs into an attic so clean and fresh she hardly recognized it. Alice began to believe in delivery.

"This bell by your bed," Bett explained, "all you need to do is ring it, and Angel will come."

Alice laughed until her coughing stopped her.

"It's a sort of miracle you're alive," Trudy said when she and Jill came home from work and up to see her.

"I'm indestructible," Alice said, a great world-weariness in her voice.

"This place was a rat's nest," Jill complained. "You can't have thrown out a paper since we moved in — or an empty yogurt carton. Is that all you eat?"

"I eat out," Alice said, "for whatever business of yours it is. And nobody asked you to clean up after me."

188

"It scared us pretty badly," Trudy said. "We all came close to being killed."

"Sometimes you remind me a little of Harriet," Alice said with slow malice. "That's a friend of mine who killed herself."

"We know who Harriet is," Jill said. "Al, if we can't talk about this, we're all going to have to move out."

"Move out? What for?"

"Because we don't want to be burned to death in our sleep."

"You've got to promise us that you won't drink when you're smoking or smoke when you're drinking," Trudy said.

"This is my house. I'm the landlady. You're the tenants," Alice announced.

"We realize that. There's nothing we can do unless you'll be reasonable."

Bett came into the room with a dinner tray.

"Get out, all of you!" Alice shouted. "And take that muck with you!"

Jill and Trudy were twins in obedience. Bett didn't budge.

"I got you out because I promised we'd feed you."

"What you eat is swill!"

"Look, Angel even cooked you some hamburger."

"You can't make conditions for me in my own house."

"I know that; so do the others. Al, I don't want to leave. I don't want to leave you. I love you. I want you to do it for yourself."

"Don't say that to me unless I'm drunk. I can't handle it."

"Yes, you can. You don't have to drink."

"What in hell else am I supposed to do to pass the time?" Alice demanded.

"Read, watch t.v., make friends, make love."

"Don't taunt me!" Alice cried into the tray of food on her lap.

"I'm not taunting," Bett said. "I want to help."

Until Alice could walk well enough to get out of the house on her own, there was no question of drinking. She kept nothing in the house, having always used drink as an excuse to escape Harriet. There was nothing to steal from her tenants. She was too proud to ask even Bett to bring her a bottle. The few cigarettes she'd brought home with her from the hospital would have to be her comfort. She found herself opening a window every time she had one and emptying and washing the ashtray when she was through.

"You're turning me into a sneak!" she shouted at Bett.

"It all looks nice and tidy to me," Bett said. "Trudy says you're so male-identified that you can't take care of yourself. I'm going to tell her she's wrong."

Alice threw a clean ashtray at her, and she ducked and laughed.

"You're getting better, you really are."

Alice returned to the beer parlor before she returned to work. She wasn't walking well, but she was walking. She had been missed. When she told about stamping out the fire with her own bare feet, she was assured of more free beer than she could drink in an evening even when she was in practice. How good it tasted and how companionable these friends who never asked questions and therefore didn't analyze the answers, who made connection with yarns and jokes. Alice had hung onto a couple of the best hospital stories and told them before she was drunk enough to lose her way or the punch line. She only laughed enough to cough at other peoples' jokes, which, as the evening wore on, were less well told and not as funny. Drink did not anesthetize the pain in Alice's healing feet, and that made her critical. Getting a tit caught in a wringer wasn't funny; it hurt.

"And here's one for those tenants of yours, Al, hey? How can you stem the tide of women's liberation? Put your finger in the dyke!"

It was an ugly face shoved into her own. Alice suddenly realized why a man must be forgiven his beard growing in the night, forgiven over and over again, too, for not being the prince of a fellow you wished he were. Alice didn't forgive. She laughed until she was near to spitting blood, finished her beer and her cigarette, and went out to find her car. As on so many other nights, even a few minutes after she got home, she couldn't remember the drive, but she knew she'd done it quietly and well.

"Come on," Bett said. "Those feet hurt. I'm going to carry you up."

Drunk in the arms of the sunny Amazon, Alice said, "Do you know how to stem the tide of women's liberation? Do you?"

"Does anyone want to?" Bett asked, making her careful, slow way up the stairs.

"Sure. Lots of people. You put your finger . . ."

"In the dyke, yeah, I know."

"Don't you think that's funny?"

"No."

"I don't either," Alice agreed.

Bett carried Alice over to her bed, which had been turned down, probably by Angel.

"Now, I want you to hand over the rest of your cigarettes," Bett said. "I'll leave them for you in the hall."

"Take them," Alice said.

191

"All right," Bett agreed and reached into Alice's blouse where she kept a pack tucked into her bra when she didn't have a pocket.

Alice half bit, half kissed the hand, then pressed herself up against those marvelous breasts, a hand on each, and felt the nipples, under the thin cloth of Bett's shirt, harden. Bett had the cigarettes, but she did not move away. Instead, with her free hand, she unbuttoned her shirt and gave Alice her dream.

As in a dream, Alice's vision floated above the scene, and she saw her own close-cropped head, hardly bigger than a baby's, her aging, liver-spotted face, her denture-deformed mouth, sucking like an obscene incubus at a young magnificence of breast which belonged to Angel. Then she saw Bett's face, serene with pity. Alice pulled herself away and spat.

"You pity me! What do you know about it? What could you know? Harriet, rest her goddamned soul, lived in *mortal sin* with me. She *killed herself* for me. It's not to *pity!* Get out! Get out, all of you right now because I'm going to burn this house down when I damned well please."

"All right," Bett said.

"It's my hell. I earned it."

"All right," Bett said, her face as bright as a never-to-come morning.

Alice didn't begin to cry until Bett had left the room, tears as hot with pain and loss as fire, that burned and burned and burned.

Acknowledgements:

"My Father's House," "Housekeeper," "In the Basement of the House," "Middle Children" and "My Country Wrong" first appeared in *The Ladder*; "House" first appeared under another title in *Redbook*; "A Walk by Himself" was published in an earlier version in *Klanak Islands* (Periwinkle Press); "If There Is No Gate" first appeared in *San Francisco Review* and was published in *Stories from Pacific and Arctic Canada* (Macmillan); "Brother and Sister" was published in '72 (Oberon); "Theme for Diverse Instruments" was published in *Contemporary Voices* (Prentice-Hall); "In The Attic Of The House" first appeared in *Christopher Street* and was reprinted in the 1981 collection, *Outlander* (Naiad Press).

A few of the publications of
THE NAIAD PRESS, INC.
P.O. Box 10543 ● Tallahassee, Florida 32302
Phone (904) 539-5965
Mail orders welcome. Please include 15% postage.

PRIORITIES by Lynda Lyons 288 pp. Science fiction with a twist. ISBN 0-941483-66-5 — $8.95

THEME FOR DIVERSE INSTRUMENTS by Jane Rule. 208 pp. Powerful romantic lesbian stories. ISBN 0-941483-63-0 — 8.95

LESBIAN QUERIES by Hertz & Ertman. 112 pp. The questions you were too embarrassed to ask. ISBN 0-941483-67-3 — 8.95

CLUB 12 by Amanda Kyle Williams. 288 pp. Espionage thriller featuring a lesbian agent! ISBN 0-941483-64-9 — 8.95

DEATH DOWN UNDER by Claire McNab. 240 pp. 3rd Det. Insp. Carol Ashton mystery. ISBN 0-941483-39-8 — 8.95

MONTANA FEATHERS by Penny Hayes. 256 pp. Vivian and Elizabeth find love in frontier Montana. ISBN 0-941483-61-4 — 8.95

CHESAPEAKE PROJECT by Phyllis Horn. 304 pp. Jessie & Meredith in perilous adventure. ISBN 0-941483-58-4 — 8.95

LIFESTYLES by Jackie Calhoun. 224 pp. Contemporary Lesbian lives and loves. ISBN 0-941483-57-6 — 8.95

VIRAGO by Karen Marie Christa Minns. 208 pp. Darsen has chosen Ginny. ISBN 0-941483-56-8 — 8.95

WILDERNESS TREK by Dorothy Tell. 192 pp. Six women on vacation learning "new" skills. ISBN 0-941483-60-6 — 8.95

MURDER BY THE BOOK by Pat Welch. 256 pp. A Helen Black Mystery. First in a series. ISBN 0-941483-59-2 — 8.95

BERRIGAN by Vicki P. McConnell. 176 pp. Youthful Lesbian–romantic, idealistic Berrigan. ISBN 0-941483-55-X — 8.95

LESBIANS IN GERMANY by Lillian Faderman & B. Eriksson. 128 pp. Fiction, poetry, essays. ISBN 0-941483-62-2 — 8.95

THE BEVERLY MALIBU by Katherine V. Forrest. 288 pp. A Kate Delafield Mystery. 3rd in a series. ISBN 0-941483-47-9 — 16.95

THERE'S SOMETHING I'VE BEEN MEANING TO TELL YOU Ed. by Loralee MacPike. 288 pp. Gay men and lesbians coming out to their children. ISBN 0-941483-44-4 — 9.95 / ISBN 0-941483-54-1 — 16.95

LIFTING BELLY by Gertrude Stein. Ed. by Rebecca Mark. 104 pp. Erotic poetry. ISBN 0-941483-51-7 — 8.95 / ISBN 0-941483-53-3 — 14.95

DOUBLE DAUGHTER by Vicki P. McConnell. 216 pp. A Nyla
Wade Mystery, third in the series.   ISBN 0-941483-26-6   8.95

HEAVY GILT by Delores Klaich. 192 pp. Lesbian detective/
disappearing homophobes/upper class gay society.
                                            ISBN 0-941483-25-8   8.95

THE FINER GRAIN by Denise Ohio. 216 pp. Brilliant young
college lesbian novel.   ISBN 0-941483-11-8   8.95

THE AMAZON TRAIL by Lee Lynch. 216 pp. Life, travel & lore
of famous lesbian author.   ISBN 0-941483-27-4   8.95

HIGH CONTRAST by Jessie Lattimore. 264 pp. Women of the
Crystal Palace.   ISBN 0-941483-17-7   8.95

OCTOBER OBSESSION by Meredith More. Josie's rich, secret
Lesbian life.   ISBN 0-941483-18-5   8.95

LESBIAN CROSSROADS by Ruth Baetz. 276 pp. Contemporary
Lesbian lives.   ISBN 0-941483-21-5   9.95

BEFORE STONEWALL: THE MAKING OF A GAY AND
LESBIAN COMMUNITY by Andrea Weiss & Greta Schiller.
96 pp., 25 illus.   ISBN 0-941483-20-7   7.95

WE WALK THE BACK OF THE TIGER by Patricia A. Murphy.
192 pp. Romantic Lesbian novel/beginning women's movement.
                                            ISBN 0-941483-13-4   8.95

SUNDAY'S CHILD by Joyce Bright. 216 pp. Lesbian athletics, at
last the novel about sports.   ISBN 0-941483-12-6   8.95

OSTEN'S BAY by Zenobia N. Vole. 204 pp. Sizzling adventure
romance set on Bonaire.   ISBN 0-941483-15-0   8.95

LESSONS IN MURDER by Claire McNab. 216 pp. 1st Det. Inspec.
Carol Ashton mystery — erotic tension!.   ISBN 0-941483-14-2   8.95

YELLOWTHROAT by Penny Hayes. 240 pp. Margarita, bandit,
kidnaps Julia.   ISBN 0-941483-10-X   8.95

SAPPHISTRY: THE BOOK OF LESBIAN SEXUALITY by
Pat Califia. 3d edition, revised. 208 pp.   ISBN 0-941483-24-X   8.95

CHERISHED LOVE by Evelyn Kennedy. 192 pp. Erotic
Lesbian love story.   ISBN 0-941483-08-8   8.95

LAST SEPTEMBER by Helen R. Hull. 208 pp. Six stories & a
glorious novella.   ISBN 0-941483-09-6   8.95

THE SECRET IN THE BIRD by Camarin Grae. 312 pp. Striking,
psychological suspense novel.   ISBN 0-941483-05-3   8.95

TO THE LIGHTNING by Catherine Ennis. 208 pp. Romantic
Lesbian 'Robinson Crusoe' adventure.   ISBN 0-941483-06-1   8.95

THE OTHER SIDE OF VENUS by Shirley Verel. 224 pp.
Luminous, romantic love story.   ISBN 0-941483-07-X   8.95

BLACK LESBIANS: AN ANNOTATED BIBLIOGRAPHY
compiled by J. R. Roberts. Foreword by Barbara Smith. 112 pp.
Award-winning bibliography.   ISBN 0-930044-21-5   5.95

THE MARQUISE AND THE NOVICE by Victoria Ramstetter.
108 pp. A Lesbian Gothic novel.   ISBN 0-930044-16-9   6.95

OUTLANDER by Jane Rule. 207 pp. Short stories and essays
by one of our finest writers.   ISBN 0-930044-17-7   8.95

ALL TRUE LOVERS by Sarah Aldridge. 292 pp. Romantic
novel set in the 1930s and 1940s.   ISBN 0-930044-10-X   7.95

A WOMAN APPEARED TO ME by Renee Vivien. 65 pp. A
classic; translated by Jeannette H. Foster.   ISBN 0-930044-06-1   5.00

CYTHEREA'S BREATH by Sarah Aldridge. 240 pp. Romantic
novel about women's entrance into medicine.
                                           ISBN 0-930044-02-9   6.95

TOTTIE by Sarah Aldridge. 181 pp. Lesbian romance in the
turmoil of the sixties.   ISBN 0-930044-01-0   6.95

THE LATECOMER by Sarah Aldridge. 107 pp. A delicate love
story.   ISBN 0-930044-00-2   6.95

ODD GIRL OUT by Ann Bannon.   ISBN 0-930044-83-5   5.95

I AM A WOMAN by Ann Bannon.   ISBN 0-930044-84-3   5.95

WOMEN IN THE SHADOWS by Ann Bannon.
                                           ISBN 0-930044-85-1   5.95

JOURNEY TO A WOMAN by Ann Bannon.
                                           ISBN 0-930044-86-X   5.95

BEEBO BRINKER by Ann Bannon.   ISBN 0-930044-87-8   5.95
          Legendary novels written in the fifties and sixties,
               set in the gay mecca of Greenwich Village.

VOLUTE BOOKS

JOURNEY TO FULFILLMENT   Early classics by Valerie   3.95

A WORLD WITHOUT MEN   Taylor: The Erika Frohmann   3.95

RETURN TO LESBOS   series.   3.95

These are just a few of the many Naiad Press titles — we are the oldest and
largest lesbian/feminist publishing company in the world. Please request a
complete catalog. We offer personal service; we encourage and welcome
direct mail orders from individuals who have limited access to bookstores
carrying our publications.